WHEN A WEALTHY THUG WANTS YOU

T'YANNA SHA-NAY

When A Wealthy Thug Wants You

Copyright © 2023 by T'yanna Sha-Nay

All rights reserved.

Published in the United States of America.

Published by Cole Hart Signature, LLC.

Mailing List

To stay up to date on new releases, plus get information on contests, sneak peeks, and more,

Go To The Website Below...

www.colehartsignature.com

This one is for that light-skinned nigga I loved to hate; I love you!
I hope you knew my heart ...

FOREVER Y can't forget the G!

KO'RAE
HE KNOWS THAT I'M HER

"Friend, why are you crying?"

With tears plaguing my vision, I couldn't see her; I could only hear her. Ahja, my best friend, had been sitting beside me in silence for that last twenty minutes and I knew her mind was wondering as to why I was crying.

"I'm just tired Ahj, I'm tired."

"Is it Greg? It's Greg, isn't it?"

She was right, she hit it right on the nose. Greg, my boyfriend, was draining me. I loved him, and it seemed like he just loved to make a fool out of me. And as much as I knew that, I didn't deserve to be continuously treated like shit or for him to just blatantly disregard my feelings time and time again. The truth was that I was way better than this entire situation, but for some strange reason I just couldn't seem to leave. It's like a part of me refused to give up after all the time, effort, and even money that I put into this relationship.

"You deserve better, Ko. That nigga is a bum."

I sat quietly, unable to refute what my best friend had just shared because a part of me agreed, even though I loved that nigga down to his dirty ass draws. Facts were facts.

"You can't keep letting him break you down like this either. You are so much better than this, damn."

Ahja despised Greg, and it wasn't always like this, she and Greg used to be cool once upon a time. It actually wasn't until he started doing me so dirty that she fell back from him, and now most days I found myself torn between my best friend and my boyfriend.

"You are the prize, Ko. Look at yourself, and I'm not just talking about your beauty; you are beautiful inside and out. Your heart is so pure, you see the good in even the worst people. Your heart is too big for your body..."

Ahja, as much drama as I put her through with my crazy life, had never turned her back on me. Everyone needed a friend like Ahja in their life. I knew my actions and wild ways hurt her deeply, she expressed it to me often. And as much as I tried to get myself together and grow up, Greg just seemed to bring me down time and time again.

I used my free hand while the other held my cellphone, the device I had just used to watch a video of the nigga I cherished hugging up on a female that wasn't me. With my free hand I wiped my tears and eventually dropped the phone.

"I bet that's him calling you now, and I bet he's so sorry for whatever he just did." Ahja rolled her eyes and still, I said nothing. Instead, I just sat in silence, staring out my apartment window in a daze.

"So, what are you going to do?" Ahja nudged me as she rested her head on my shoulder. I cried even harder now because I knew that she saw me, she witnessed me in so much pain, and I felt like I let her down time and time again.

"What did he even do?" She shot question after question at me, only I was truly too tired, too drained, too hurt to even respond.

With my head rested against the wall as Ahja held my hand with her head rested on my shoulder, together the two of us sat in more silence. Not only was Greg out with another bitch last night, but his ass was also with THE very same bitch that he told me he didn't mess with or even know. He talked so much shit about the bitch that I should've known it was too good to be true. My gut told me so, I knew it. My intuition was always on point yet someway, somehow, I continued to play victim to my own situation and ignore the signs.

"Rae, we need to get up before your mother gets home. Let's go take a ride and get something to eat, a drink, or something. I'll drive if you don't feel up to it."

My mother was the sweetest woman until she wasn't. She raised me and my two brothers the best she could. I wasn't sure if it was because I was her only daughter that I got it the worst, but my brothers could literally do no wrong in her eyes. My mother and I went at it so frequently it was so hard to feel her love most days. She showed no emotion toward me, no affection, yet my brothers got it all. Thank God for my daddy though. Even though he wasn't around as much I still felt his love even with him miles away.

Approximately three to five minutes later, I got up and decided to suck it up.

"I'm going to shower," I told Ahja as I looked down at my series 8 Apple Watch to check the time. My mother would be home soon and if she witnessed me sitting around crying about Greg, she'd throw a fit. Just like Ahja, my mother was tired of the back and forth he and I were into.

"Good, now get your funky ass in the shower, get dressed, and we're going to go out. Fuck Greg."

"We are too young, too cute, and too lit to be stressing over these raggedy ass niggas. I cut Orin off and it's time for you to let Greg's ass go too. We deserve so much more, friend. We're only twenty-eight and have been through shit worth a lifetime just being with niggas who mean us no damn good."

"He didn't start out like this, Ahj." I tried to reason with her, and she sucked her teeth.

"I look at you sideways every time you make an excuse for that nigga and not because I'm being shady, it's just because I can't believe that you don't see what I see. You hated me constantly going back and forth with Orin for so many years and now it's like damn bitch how you end up in the same situation..."

The disappointment in her voice was evident, it filled my tiny room with ease. It's what caused us to be distant for days. I didn't even bother looking her in her eyes because I already knew what they would say. I knew they were disheartened. I could vividly see my best friend without even looking at her that's how often we had been down this road before. I didn't blame her, I felt it too, I was hurting too. I just didn't know how to come up off this nigga.

"I don't know," I expressed as I pulled my knotless braids to the back of my head and out my face before heading toward the bathroom. My braids were way past my butt, almost to my knees. I had just gotten my hair braided yesterday, excited to be off the very next day. Excited to be going out with Ahj and our longtime friend Gia. Nowhere in my plans did I have time scheduled for me to be sulking over this nigga.

Thankfully, I kept my hair done. It was just something about having a new hairstyle that made me feel good. It was one of the constant things in my life that I looked forward to, getting fly and keeping my hair neat.

Standing here lost in my thoughts, I looked around my mom's three-bedroom apartment in Brooklyn where I had lived my entire life with my mother and two brothers. My brother Nine had been in and out of the penitentiary since he was seventeen, he was the oldest. I couldn't remember the last time my brother lived under my mother's roof. Nine was the problem kid yet he did no wrong in my mother's eyes as he wreaked mayhem all over Brooklyn and its neighboring boroughs. Then there was Elias, who I called Eli, he was the baby, he was my baby. I had basically raised him with my mother working long hours at the hospital the last sixteen years to provide for her family. Eli was my everything; he was nothing like Nine or me for that matter. He was in love with reading, writing, and sports. If it wasn't basketball, it was football and thanks to Nine, he was able to attend every training camp that his heart desired. He always had the latest everything, sneakers, clothes, coats, you name it, Eli had it thanks to Nine. One thing I could say about my big brother despite his demonic ways, he spoiled us rotten. Even at twenty-eight if I called my brother for two or even three thousand dollars, it was mine, no questions asked. Nine spoiled us with no complaints. He was the reason that I was able to get my car. I really wanted a Benz, but I had to settle for a Honda though. He humbled me real quick after an argument we had, still he paid the down payment for my car and made sure that my insurance was paid every month. Nine kept me fly. Even with me working down at the clinic at the hospital where my mother worked, still my big brother made sure I had everything I wanted. Givenchy Shark Lock Boots, Rick Owens, Prada, Nike, Dior, Chanel, you name it and Nine made it happen. Majority of my money went to food, gas, and just whatever I wanted, to be honest.

"Ko'rae, hurry up in the bathroom." I heard my mother's sweet voice on the other side of the door and sighed.

Damn, I just got in here for real.

"Okay," I responded while I grabbed my Method Body Wash Pure Peace and applied it to my exfoliating rag once more. Usually, I took about thirty minutes in the shower but today I had to be done in fifteen with my mother home from work. On one hand, I was way beyond ready to move out and on the other hand, I wanted to spend as much time with my mother and little brother as I could because they were important to me. I had been apartment hunting for about a year and a half now and my mom was so against it. Even with Nine being almost thirty she still wanted him home. She wanted all her babies under the same roof.

I was thankful that my hair was braided and I wasn't wearing it in its natural state, because the steam from the bathroom was sure to frizz it up. My mixed genes were a gift and a curse. My mother's Guyanese background and my father's African American bloodline left me mixed with a head full of long, curly hair.

As time passed, I knew that it was time for me to get out before she came back tripping on me. Instead of wallowing in my feelings, I gathered my things in the bathroom to bring them back to my bedroom. On my walk down the tiled hallway, I overheard my mother and Ahja talking as they usually would. Ahja was not only my best friend she was my godsister. Her mother, Diane, was also my godmother and when she passed five years ago due to domestic violence, my mom made sure that Ahja was well taken care of. Ahja's mom and my father were best friends almost all their lives. They grew up in Edgemere projects together, then Diane met my mom back in '92, a few years before me and Ahja were born, and they became inseparable. Diane used to always tell me and Ahja the tea on their past. It was because of Diane that I knew how my parents met and fell in love. Diane was one of those moms you didn't come by often. She was strict, yet she still made us feel comfortable to be ourselves around her. School was always a top priority for her and my mom. It was them who pushed us to go away to college to further our education.

"Where y'all going?" My mother, Kimora Sanders, stood leaning on the doorframe of my bedroom waiting for one of us to give her an answer.

I ran my hands through my knotless braids as I separated my hair, creating the perfect side part. I had just laid my edges to perfection too, and with the right amount of lip gloss I never had to do much to look my best. I always knew I was *that* girl. I had just pulled my white cropped Zara t-shirt over my head and adjusted the white-gold letter K necklace my father brought me years ago and looked myself over in my full-length mirror while I fastened the button to my favorite pair of black jeans. While I admired my reflection, I straightened out my hair so it could fall down my back neatly and smiled as I looked myself over in the mirror. My wide hips and thick thighs all came from my mother. I was literally the spitting image of her.

"Ko'rae, get out that damn mirror," my mother spoke from

the doorway, and I pulled myself away from my reflection, giving her my undivided attention.

My mother was a Guyanese woman who was born and raised in Guyana until the age of fifteen. She was so beautiful, her long silky hair hung down her back while being parted down the middle. She had a mole on her left cheek that only enhanced her beautiful face. Sometimes when I looked into her eyes, I saw myself so clear. My mom had beauty like Nia Long and Sanaa Lathan in the 90's, like that natural fresh face beauty, and she passed it all down to me and my brothers. Like my mother, I had rich, flawless skin. I inherited her genes from head to toe with pride.

Standing at 5 foot 5, with bright brown eyes, I could see the resemblance through the mirror and it kind of made me smile because to me, my mother was one of the most beautiful women in the world.

"I swear you have her whole face." Ahja would always say this, and it was true. It was so true that sometimes when we went out my mother and I were often mistaken for being twins.

"She wishes she could look this good, Ahja. Don't be out all late having me worrying, please. I'm working a double, so I need some sleep."

"Where's Eli?" I asked, just now noticing that he didn't come in like he usually did with my mom.

"He's staying with your brother this weekend. I thought I told you that. Nine picked him up early from school for some training session."

"Oh, that's this weekend. I'll sleep with Ahj tonight since you're working a double."

"Okay. Can you please call and text me so that I know you two are safe? Lock the door," my mother shouted over her shoulder as she walked off to her bedroom across the hall from mine.

"Greg who? Bitch, you look the fuck good." Ahja complimented me, and I gave her one right back.

With the passing of Diane, Ahja was left the responsibility of her mother's apartment. At the tender age of twenty-three, she was forced to grow up something serious. And living on her own the last four years weren't easy, but Ahj had been handling everything the best she could. From twenty-three to now she had grown so much, we both had. Together we had been through everything, we went through it all... from her mom passing, my dad being sent to the feds and my family losing almost everything, Nine going to prison, and us almost having to move into the shelter before my mom got called for her apartment. If I didn't have Ahja, there was no telling where I'd be right now. I know for sure I probably never would have finished college without her. We beat the odds together, and I couldn't have asked for a better person to go through life with.

"Rae, you good?" Ahja looked over at me while we sat at a red light. She was driving and I was sitting across from her lost in my thoughts. We were on our way to Mojo for some food and drinks. Even if I wasn't in my feelings, I still don't think I'd be up to driving. I really had to be in the mood to drive most days. It wasn't at all what it was cracked up to be to me.

"Greg again?" Ahja asked me as I looked down at my phone ringing.

"No, it's Nine." As I sat there in the passenger seat watching my brother's handsome face sit on my screen, I had to muster up some energy to answer the phone for him. Nine was thirty and he was the spitting image of our father with the perfect mix of our mother. His six-foot-three stature towered over me and his smile lit up a room. To know him was to love him, only there was also another side to my brother that you didn't want to meet.

"Hello."

"Yo, why niggas saying ya boy out here with some next bitch?"

"Where you at?"

"The hood, I just left Eli's practice, but my niggas called putting me on. What's good with that nigga, ya broke up?"

"No."

"So, you just letting niggas play in your face?"

Every hair rose on my body as my brother spoke. I was embarrassed. This nigga was constantly embarrassing me, leaving our business in the streets and forcing me to have hard conversations with the people I loved the most.

"No."

"Handle that shit Rae, niggas only going to do what you allow. I been telling you that. I can't live your life for you. If you can't see how this nigga treating you ain't right, then that's on you and maybe you deserve it. Stupid ass."

CLICK!

Tears threatened to fall from my eyes once the phone disconnected. The phone was on speaker so Ahja heard everything.

"Let's go to Steinway." I broke the silence and suggested a new location as opposed to Mojo. Prior to me being in my feelings, Ahja and I had plans to go to Gia's outing for her birthday at this lounge on Steinway.

"Rae, are you sure?"

"Yes. There's nothing I can do right now. Greg is clearly going to keep doing what the fuck he wants." Inhaling, I took a deep breath and allowed my eyes to roll. I rolled my eyes hard and sucked in air once more before exhaling as I attempted to calm my nerves.

"Okay then, we're about to turn the fuck up, but you have to deal with that. You can't just run from it."

"I don't know what to do, Ahja. I tried leaving, I set boundaries, the nigga just keeps finding his way back. Right now, I just want to be. I'm not about to fuck up my day over an unfaithful ass nigga."

My sense of hurt usually outweighed logic. I usually would run and hide in a corner until Greg came back begging me to forgive him. Nah, those days had to be behind me. I had to put my foot down or else he was only going to continue to hurt me. Nine was right, I was being stupid. I knew better yet I continued to settle because I was comfortable. Greg was my comfort zone. I was complacent and I needed to get out of that.

"Gia is going to be so happy that we're coming. She damn near cried when I told her we weren't going to be able to make it."

"Yeah, I was tripping. I don't know what I was thinking. Fuck Greg, I'm outside tonight. I'll deal with that when I deal with it. If I even feel like it."

Ahja nodded as she cleared the GPS and put in the address to our new location. I placed my phone between my legs and pulled the visor down to reapply my lip gloss. I wasn't the least bit worried about being underdressed because even on a calm day I was still HER. The white cropped shirt and black jeans I wore were topped off with my favorite Rick Owens DRKSHDW, I had about three pair. The black and white ones were my favorite.

I love you Rae.

The text from my little brother brought warmth to my body. Eli will always and forever be my soft spot. He always seemed to come through when I needed him the most. I knew he had to be close by when Nine called me, and I hated that he ever had to witness any of my mistakes. I couldn't understand how this nigga damn near trapped me to be with him and he couldn't do right.

You have to get your shit together, Rae. It's not looking good. Are you a weak bitch?

My thoughts were consuming me. There was this constant battle in my mind as I tried to figure out what the hell to do next. It's like I could leave Greg alone, I knew that I had it in me, it was just when I wanted what I wanted, I didn't care about anything. Sometimes I craved that nigga, like I wanted to be in his skin, that's how bad he had me at times. I was hung up on the thought of him, for sure, not because of who he was right now. The nigga I had, at least the version of him that I had, wasn't worth shit. I knew that, I wasn't delusional. I was just stubborn and selfish. I held on to Greg for my own selfish reasons.

When Ahja and I pulled up to Crystal Lounge there was a line outside and it was long. Gia was one of those people who knew everybody. She was lit on social media, in every borough, she was just one of those girls that everyone got along with, and I wasn't the least bit surprised to see that so many people had come out to celebrate with her.

"Raeeeeee!" Gia yelled my name once she spotted me coming across the street.

"Happy birthday!" We hugged before she gave Ahja the same attention.

"They're with me," Gia spoke to the man at the door, and we were allowed in with ease. We could hear the murmurs and complaints from everyone left outside on the line.

"Look at all of them fake bitches trying to get in." Gia laughed as we made our way to her section.

"I'm so happy that *my* bitches came through for me though. Y'all know that you two are my turn-up partners, it's no party without you two bitches."

Gia grabbed a bottle of Don Julio and handed it to Ahja. Ahja got straight to it, pouring us each shots, and I was ready to let the night begin. To think just hours ago I was sitting on my living room floor crying my eyes out over a nigga. Pathetic.

"Fuck Greg." I took my shot with ease and handed my cup back to Ahja for another one.

"There's so many niggas in here tonight. Damn," Gia let out over the music, and I began to scan the room. She was right, the niggas were out. Amiri Denim, Dior, Gallery DEPT, APs, Cuban link chains. I had no complaints as I surveyed the men in Gia's section.

"Gia, who the fuck is that?" Ahja nudged Gia as the three of us were finishing off the bottle of Don Julio and vibing to the music.

"Bitch, who? Where?" Gia took a long pull from the hookah and released a big cloud of white smoke before passing it to me.

"Over there, the nigga in the Balenciaga hoodie." I followed Ahja's eyes to see who she was talking about because there were plenty of men in here that looked good. Hell, I had my eyes on a few.

"Oh, that's Loui, with his fine ass."

"Bitch, who don't you know?" Ahja joked, because Gia knew everyone.

"I know all the niggas with the money too. Loui is cool peoples. He's from Queens, I think Rockaway."

"Like Far Rockaway?" Ahja screwed her face up and we all shared a laugh.

"Don't do them like that. You know the first nigga I ever loved was from Far Rock. That nigga was the shit. I'm waiting on him to come home to jump right back on that nigga."

"Who? Not the nigga with the girlfriend. Not the nigga you didn't start taking serious until he got locked up. It can't be that nigga."

"Girlfriend, bitch please. Snatchiesssssss. And we did start getting serious once he got locked up. It's something about niggas in jail, they can lead a fish out of water, bitch."

"Gia, you are a fool."

"For real. Kash and i were always cool but it's like once he got locked up, he started... I don't know, it was just different."

"Yeah, because he's in jail, Gia. Be fucking for real."

"I know Rae..."

"I'm just saying, be careful. Because he's in jail he'll tend to say all the right things. That's usually how it goes. There's a reason why you didn't give him a chance while he was home is all I'm saying, so don't be a fool for no nigga in jail who's probably fucking with you and ten other bitches the same way."

"I'm not stupid, Rae. I know how this goes but I care about Kash. We were always friends first. I know that I may scream '*my man, my man, my man,*' but trust me, I'm on to his ass. I'm just playing my role accordingly. Plus, Kash takes care of me. Do you think that I could do all that I do and buy all that I have off my salary? Hell no! With Kash, I don't pay bills, I don't pay for anything, to be honest. Kash buys my clothes, my groceries, my shoes, my bags, he does everything and in return, all I have to do is answer the phone."

"Well, since you put it that way, do you then, girl. Just be careful," I warned, because I knew firsthand how it was for niggas in jail. They'd love you up until the day they came home. I watched my brother do it time and time again.

"But back to Loui's fine ass. Look, he has almost every bitch in here drooling. Including Ahja's ass." Gia noticeably took the attention off herself and placed it on Ahja as the three of us watched him from a distance. The man was fine, I'd give him that.

"I mean, he looks good but I'm not no thirsty bitch."

"Ahja, trust me, I know a thirsty hoe when I see one, but Loui is one of them niggas that likes to flash his money to reel a bitch in and hide his paper once he gets you where he wants you. You know I know all the hood niggas' business. The ones with money at least." A dose of Gia was just what I needed to get out my head and my feelings.

"You act just like a nigga sometimes," I chimed in as I scanned the dimly lit establishment. The shots were slowly kicking in and I was starting to have a good time.

I was big *fuck Greg* right now.

"Rae, we're about to find you a finer nigga with way more money, fuck Greg!"

It was almost like Gia was reading my mind with the way she spoke exactly what I was thinking.

"If she's even really ready for all that, G. I'm not even sure she's single, you know how she gets..." Ahja never missed a beat when it came to throwing shade my way about Greg, and truthfully, I couldn't blame her, because if anyone knew how wishy washy I was when it came to Greg, it was her. Plus, Ahja was always going to say she how felt.

I tuned Ahja out with the music and decided that tonight Greg was going to be the least of my worries. I was out here to have a good time with my girls, not cry over my trifling ass boyfriend.

"Oh bitch, trust me, I'm single," I let out once my eyes landed on the very last person I expected to see in here with another bitch.

"For a nigga with no money and no time, he sure seems to have both right now." Ahja threw another jab while I felt my body temperature rise.

BRIXX

THEY KNOW THAT I'M THOROUGH

"Yo Brixx, you need to see this shit."

"What's that?" I asked as I pulled my eyes from my phone. I had been checking my email all night in hopes the owner of the club in Houston hit me back. When I finally looked up, my eyes landed on shorty with the Rick Owens' on. I was unsure if she was who or what he was referring to, but she for sure had my attention.

"Who that?" I tapped him to bring his attention to where I was looking.

"Damn, she bad and she with Gia. I'm about to go see what's up."

We had been looking for Gia since we walked in. It was her birthday and we planned on surprising her tonight, but it looked like she was the one surprising us.

"Hell yeah, that's Gia and it looks like she's about to get into some shit." Shaking my head, I waited. I knew Eazy like the back of my hand, so I was mentally preparing myself to talk him out of whatever he was thinking of doing. Tonight wasn't the night to get into some shit, we were just supposed to come out and show Gia some love.

My eyes landed on Gia and shorty with the Rick Owens', and

by their body language I could tell that their conversation with dude wasn't positive.

Of course, the one female that I saw tonight that was easy on the eyes was into it with some nigga. My luck was funny like that. She was beautiful though, thick, and juicy. She had the cutest set of eyes that I've seen in quite some time.

"I know that nigga didn't just put his hand on shorty..." Eazy was my right hand and had been since high school. He was more like my brother than anything.

Gia was like family. We'd known her since we were kids growing up in Long Island City up until her family moved across town to Brooklyn, and Eazy had always been the type to shoot first and ask questions later for situations with less merit than this.

Once he stood up with his eyes locked on Gia and her friends, I knew it was too late to talk him out of anything.

"Yo, don't go over there, my nigga." I tried stopping him, but it was too late.

I let out a sigh and trotted behind him with confidence. I knew whatever Eazy decided to do that I was standing behind him one hundred percent. Right or wrong, I was riding with my boy.

We were just two niggas from the bottom who had hustled our way to the top and loyalty was what we stood on.

Following his lead, I stood from the section we had in the small lounge.

Just this morning I flew in from DC after kicking it with my family for a few days, and I was happy to be back in NY. There was nothing like the love this city gave me. As an out-of-town nigga, I had been coming back and forth to NY since I was a kid, being that my pops was born and raised out here.

"Rae, no!" was all we heard before the commotion started.

"Oh shit, shorty wilding on that nigga." Eazy stopped dead in his tracks just as he approached where Gia and her friends were beating on some nigga.

Shorty in the Rick's was doing the most damage. That's when

it clicked. It was personal for her, it had to be with the way she was beating on ol' boy.

"Yo nah, this looks like some domestic shit, I'm out." I tapped Eazy and instantly turned around. I wasn't the nigga to stand around and wait for shit to escalate, I got low instantly. All that drama was for the niggas who didn't have anything to lose. I had way too much on the line to stand around and risk it all over a situation that didn't have a damn thing to do with me.

Damn, shorty was fine as hell though.

I shook my head as I watched Gia and another girl jump in the fight. It wasn't long before they were being escorted out by security, and the nigga was left leaking after being hit over the head with a bottle.

"Yo, shorty look good as fuck and she got hands. My kind of woman," Eazy bragged as we headed back to our section.

"Which one?" It wouldn't be the first time we saw a beautiful woman and were both attracted to her. One thing I could say is that me and my nigga never fell out over no female.

"Both of them, my nigga." Eazy shrugged as he watched Gia and her friends laugh about what they had just done as if they weren't the cause of all the commotion going on back inside.

"She fine but damn, why she fronted on that nigga like that?" I asked, even though I knew he was just as lost as me.

"Probably her nigga. He must not know that there's niggas like you and me ready to snatch shorty up."

I agreed with him while I watched from the distance, admiring shorty. I was lowkey disappointed in her too. As fine as she was, she showed me that she had some hood in her. She reminded me of a Nia Long type, like her beauty was that undeniable, natural.

Her waist was slim, her thighs were thick. She had to be about 5'5, maybe 5'6, no taller than that, brown skin. She was well put together and she had my full attention.

"You know I love drama, nigga. I'm about to go holla at her

friend. Don't think I didn't peep you either nigga, I see you watching shorty."

"Bro, you just saw what I saw, and you want to bring your slow ass over there and start with them, why?"

"Fuck it, why not?" He shrugged and I opted out on following him over to where they were talking with security. I left Eazy to pop his shit and I went to get the car from across the street and pulled up beside them.

We had already paid for our bottles so there was no need for me to chase the server down to pay our tab. I even tipped her nicely when she brought them out. And like the ignorant nigga Eazy was, he grabbed the unopened bottle of Don Julio and Casamigos and headed toward the exit. I dared somebody to say anything to him because that nigga was bound to violate.

"Yo Gia, what up, why ya do that nigga like that?" Eazy walked right over to Gia and her two friends while I played the cut.

"Eazy! Oh my god, I didn't think you were coming."

"Yeah, we pulled up just in time to see ya beat that nigga ass. What happened?"

"It's a long story. We're good now though."

"That's what's up, so we hitting the next spot or what? You know Brixx is about to take over that lounge in Queens, we could pull up there."

"I heard. Where is his stuck-up ass at?"

"In the car. What up y'all," Eazy spoke to Gia's friends while I sat in the car listening from afar.

"Rae, Ahja, this is my brother, Eazy. Eazy, *the girls.*"

Both the girls were standing just a few feet away, going back and forth exchanging words, not paying Eazy any mind.

"What up Mike Tyson and Holyfield, ya straight?"

"We're good. That nigga, on the other hand, I don't know." Gia laughed like what they had just done was cool. It had to be personal though, because they did that nigga dirty. They violated and never touched the female he was with.

"So ya pulling up or the night is over?"

"The night might be over for me but y'all can go. I'm aggravated."

"I guess another time Eazy, we had a crazy ass night."

"I feel you. Hit me, you know niggas got mad love for you G."

I watched Eazy peel off a few hundred-dollar bills and handed them to Gia. He wished her a happy birthday and made his way back over to me.

"Brixx, you could speak too, nigga," Gia yelled out playfully, and I gave her a head nod and a smile.

"You know it's all love Gia, you good? Get up with me later on."

"I will. Maybe my homegirl will calm down and we'll meet y'all there."

"A'ight, bet."

We watched them cross the street and hop in a silver, tinted Honda Accord before pulling off and going our way.

"New York, I'm back baby!" Eazy had his body hanging halfway out the window and yelled out with no regard for the pedestrians. When I say my nigga had no act right, I meant it. He was a wild boy. He was also a nigga that I'd lay it all on the line for too, no questions asked.

Placing the rolled blunt to my lips, I sparked it before I inhaled. I released the smoke through my nose and repeated the act as I drove back to Queens. A nigga stayed rolling up nothing but the best weed. I had that good shit, not that blockwork most niggas were smoking trying to pass it for some exotic gas. My man uptown had the best weed connect.

Me and Eazy clicked because the nigga had a hustler's spirit that mimicked mine.

"Yo, my nigga, why your bitch keep hitting my line looking for you?"

"My bitch?" I screwed my face up at him because Eazy knew better than to ever play disrespect with me, so it wasn't that. It was because whoever he was talking about wasn't mine. I was a single man.

"Yeah nigga, your *bitch*. At least that's what she's saying." He laughed hard as hell as he showed me the missed calls and many messages from the unsaved number in his phone.

"I would block the bitch but for what? She's only going to find a new number to harass me from. She is sick in the head, my nigga, word."

"She ain't my bitch." I tossed that out there casually because Eazy was going to pop his shit regardless. He knew what was up with me when it came to Neesha. She violated, and I was too thorough of a nigga to ever let some hoe shit slide.

It was like once I started coming into my own, everything started going downhill. Kash got locked up, Neesha started acting like owed her something, and all that I did wasn't worth shit. Neesha showed me her true colors once and that was all I needed to see. No amount of history in the world could ever make me mess with a female that wasn't loyal. I couldn't trust her, so all the begging, crying, and pleading she was doing for forgiveness was falling on the ears of a nigga who didn't give a fuck, and I was that nigga.

Once you crossed me, you lost me.

"I can't believe Neesha's fine ass was grimy like that. She was who I used to think you were going to marry."

"Marry? Nah, I'm not even going to front, me too. She violated though, fuck her."

"Word, fuck that grimy bitch." Eazy shrugged as he inhaled from his own personal blunt. That nigga used way too much grabba for me to smoke with him, so I passed.

Neesha was my heart at one point. She was someone that I trusted with my life, my bread, and my freedom because she was my bitch, someone who I would do anything for, and she violated. She fucked another nigga behind my back while I was doing a lil' six-month bid. Whole time she claimed to be this down ass bitch, but she wasn't. What got me was that I really took the time to love her ass, I tried with her, and in the end, she violated. She broke my trust, fucked some money up because she felt a nigga was going to be sitting behind bars for some time. Her stupid ass let a nigga get a hold of her phone, and that's when everything she had been doing behind my back came to the light. That night I wanted to murder her; on everything I loved, I did. I never had a female break my heart. I felt she was no longer worthy of living after being disloyal to me. I couldn't bring myself to do it. I wasn't that nigga, I was a get-money nigga, I wasn't no killer. After going through her phone, I found out all I needed to know and just like that, I left. I left her right where she was at and focused on business.

Fuck Neesha.

I looked down at my phone to check for the message from Gia.

"Yo, I told her about your spot. I don't know why you didn't just tell her to pull up there from the jump."

"Because I'm still getting shit together over there. We could pull up there though."

I was still in negotiations with the current owner, but we were close to settling on a price that we both could live with.

I handed Eazy my phone so that he could tell her what he wanted. I was with whatever, the night was still young, and a nigga came out to have a good time.

"I'm proud of you, bro. And what's up with that Houston spot? I'm trying to slide out there for the summer too."

"That's in the works too. I want everything!"

"Rich nigga shit. I remember when we used to share Pelle's and Mormont's. Look at us now!"

"Word."

Eazy held his hand out to dap me and I accepted the gesture. Unlike Eazy, I was done with the game. While he had one foot in and one foot out, I was washing my hands with the streets and focusing on bigger and better things.

"Yo, Gia dubbed it, she said shorty not feeling it. You could swing by the Diner or something, a nigga is hungry."

"Fuck I look like? Ya chauffer?"

"You look like my brother, nigga. Matter fact, I'll just slide through my shorty crib. What you about to fuck with?"

"I'm going to hit the crib, chill, play the game."

"You need to find you some business of your own, my nigga. Neesha got your head so fucked up nigga, you don't even be catching all the ass that's being thrown at you out here. Leaving a humble nigga like myself to catch 'em."

"Do you playa, I'm chilling."

"Yo, Gia said she's going to hit us tomorrow with plans."

"Tell Gia to sit her as down somewhere." I shook my head, already knowing that she was going to want us to come out tomorrow, no question.

"Hold on, I heard Gia say some funny shit earlier. You think she's still messing around with that nigga Kash?"

"Nah, she can't be, that nigga ain't been the same since he lost his sister."

"That nigga ain't never been right and we know that first-hand. How a real street nigga like him end up bitching up over some shit we all did?"

"Nigga just mad because he got caught. Fuck that nigga though, the best thing that ever happened for us was when he got locked up. Kash was one grimy nigga."

"What's crazy is how we used to look up to son. That was one pump-faking ass nigga, and now I bet he has Gia's nose wide open thinking she's fucking with a real nigga when he's just a grimy street nigga."

"Look bro, Kash is the least of our worries. Fuck him, and if Gia is still fucking with him then so be it. I've never been the type of nigga to step on another man's toes."

I was leaving well enough alone because nine times out of ten, Gia was still entertaining him, and I didn't want her feeling like she had to pick sides.

"Copy."

I dropped Eazy off in Brooklyn then headed to the crib. I didn't mind living in my condo in Astoria when I had a house in Houston. It was something about the city view that I loved, and the motivation I got living in high-rise apartment buildings that I used to dream about as a kid when I lived just a couple block away in Ravenswood projects. My pops was born and raised in Long Island City, and once him and my moms finally got it together I moved from DC to Ravenswood projects in '94.

I used to dream of living this lavish, now I had everything that I ever wanted and then some. Hard work and dedication got me here. I paid four bands a month in rent here, proudly, no longer having to rob Peter to pay Paul. A nigga was on now, paid, having his way, with his own motion. I had come a long way from the lil' nigga on the street corner selling nickel and dime bags of weed and coke. I was that nigga now, niggas fucked with me so hard because they knew that I was thorough. I was a man that stood on values, principles, and morals. I was a man who didn't play about his bread.

Brixx, I'm serious about tomorrow, that nigga fucked our night up. I need a do over.

When I got to the crib, there was another message from Gia.

I got you sis. Who shorty though?

I threw caution to the wind to see if Gia was willing to help a nigga out or if I was going to have to do all the work myself.

Which one?

Shorty with the braids and the Ricks.

Oh Rae, that's my bitch. Why, what's up?

Nun, see y'all tomorrow. Everything on me!

She sent back some emoji and I ended the conversation there.

THE NEXT DAY

"Brixx, thank you so much!"

Gia was standing on the couch and yelling over the music, leaving me hardly being able to hear her.

"You're welcome."

"You don't have to be all modest either, Brixx. This is a big deal, congratulations!"

"Appreciate it."

"You've always been humble. It's what set you apart from everyone else..."

"Gia, you drunk."

"I know, but I'm not stupid. I really am proud of you. And it's still my birthday so drink up!"

"Happy birthday." I raised the bottle of 1942 to hers and took a shot with her.

"And you're not slick, I see you looking around. I know you're looking for Rae."

"Who?"

"Don't play dumb."

"I don't know what you're talking about, G."

"Yeah, okay." She waved me off and I wondered if it was that obvious that I was peeping the crowd for shorty.

The vibe tonight was chill, way better than last night. Gia had about five other females with her in a section full of get-money niggas. Any nigga with me held his own and had his own.

"Why you think that though?"

"Oh, so you're really looking for her? And because you asked about her last night, and you don't ask about anybody."

"She look good." I shrugged and took another drink from the bottle clutched in my right hand.

"Oh, she looks good. That's it... Don't downplay my bitch."

"What you mean? You expect me to be on her dick or something?"

"Exactly! I don't know why men always try to play it cool.

Just admit it, she's fine, you're feeling her."

"I don't even know her."

"Hmm, since when did that stop you?"

"You must have me mistaken for that nigga." I nodded in Eazy's direction where he was across the section smiling in the face of every female he came across.

Meek Mill blasted through the speakers of *my* lounge, and damn did it feel good to be standing in the middle of my spot. Bottles were flowing, the room was packed damn near, and the vibe was chill as fuck. I caught eyes with Eazy across the room and he raised his bottle to me, and I did the same in return. I used to pray for times like this.

"You did it, nigga!" Eazy shouted over the music, and I nodded. Without him, there would be no me. Eazy had my back from the very first day I came outside and had been solid ever since. I never had to question his loyalty, not once, and it was because of him that I was able to maneuver through the city the way that I did, doing all that I did.

"Nah, we did it." He would never accept it, but niggas like Eazy made it so niggas like me could do what they do. I flooded the streets with the best product, I made the moves that the average man was afraid to make. I took big risks to reap an even bigger reward. Bigger risks than any nigga before me, bigger than my pops, bigger than Kash. I was going to be bigger than Meech. Money had been coming in steady ever since Kash went away. For a nigga who used to be like a brother to me, I wouldn't dare break bread with him ever again. Kash was the epitome of greedy, and he wasn't meant to lead young, hungry niggas like me and Eazy. With Kash out the way we were eating, we had it all. Money, clothes, hoes, respect, cars, even cribs in our names. He may have put us on but he didn't hold us down. Kash was a street nigga, all he knew was the streets, so in return he had no end game but me, I wanted out this shit for good. The fear of ending up like him and even my pops taunted me daily. Kash was locked up and my

pops was still hustling because he felt the streets were his only
way out.

I made millions on the streets hustling and making smart
investments. While other niggas were blowing money on cars,
clothes, and hoes, I was investing. The pipeline was mine once
Kash got knocked and I used it to my advantage. Now I was one
move away from being done with the streets for good and leaving
it all behind me. I loved the nightlife. I used to promote parties
back in the day too and that got me connections most niggas my
age would have fumbled. What started off as a hobby, just
wanting to be in the littest parties, ended up being my lifeline out
the game. I had already blown up in Houston, DC, and Philly
from my club promoting days and moving weight. I was looking
to open my own spot in Houston then DC and maybe even
Miami. If all went well with this spot, then I would have the green
light to open up however many lounges I wanted to. Most busi-
nesses failed within the first year. If I could stand the test of time
on my own, then it was up from here. I was already in the process
of heading to Houston and opening up a lounge out there with
my cousin. I made a promise to myself that once I finally started
touching grown man money that I would open the hottest clubs
in the hottest cities.

"Yo, I'm happy for you bro, and I'm glad that you decided to
come back home. DC ain't you, nigga. This is where you belong,
right here. NY is home!"

"I appreciate you, bro."

"This is you, all this." Eazy pointed around the establishment
with his bottle. "Me, I'm a real street nigga. Hustling is all I
know."

"You could have all this too." I waved him off because Eazy
was steady downplaying himself. He let words from niggas like
Kash resonate in his head that he would never be more than a
dope boy.

I had no desire to watch my brother die on the streets. We had
given up enough already. We had the funds, we had everything we

needed to leave the game. Together. Eazy didn't have to sell dope anymore but because he loved the streets so much, he couldn't see himself doing anything else. Eazy wasn't as invested in the night life like I was. I mean, yeah, he loved to party and being the nigga in the club popping the most bottles, but the business side to it all was never his thing. My nigga could rap though, and he used to back in the day. I knew if there was one thing he'd take serious outside of the streets, it was music. I was working on something for him, my boy deserved it.

"Aye, there shorty go."

"Who?" I asked before I laid eyes on her.

"Gia always has some fine ass friends. How they both look good."

Shorty was bad as fuck. She had that Nia Long and Meagan Good beauty, pretty face, natural body. Any nigga in his right mind felt what I felt when he looked at her.

"You better go talk to her before one of these thirsty niggas get at her." Eazy thought he was playing mind games on me, but I was always ten steps ahead.

"And she fly as fuck," he added as he continued to coach me into speaking to her.

"There go my bitches right there," Gia stood behind me shouting from the couch for her friends' attention.

Tonight, Rae was looking just as good as she did last night, if not better. She had on a bag and a pair of shoes that cost a grip. The price of her shoes alone was what most niggas saw on their paychecks, maybe. Then she had the Chanel bag to match the Chanel sneakers.

Rae stood out in a room full of people. As she approached the section, I caught her eye and she didn't look away, I liked that. I liked the way she smiled at whatever her friend was telling her and keeping eye contact with me. I took a shot back just before she approached us. I was grateful Gia had been at my side all night.

"You fucking up my furniture," I joked as Gia hopped off the couch, and on the walk-up she had them taking shots, then she had them take another for being late.

"Bitch, can I breathe? Damn." Her friend shot her a look as she prepared to take another shot.

"Hell no. Drink up." She handed them their third shot, and even with all the shit they popped they both threw them back with ease.

Damn.

"You make me sick, bitch. Hi," her friend spoke, and I gave her a head nod.

"What up."

"Don't mind this nigga, he's being shy or whatever. Brixx, these are my girls, Rae and Ahja."

"Heyy." Rae waved happily, causing a nigga to smile.

"Why isn't he drinking?" Ahja asked, and before I could respond Gia was handing me a shot.

"He thinks he's too cool. I guess because he's the boss..."

I gave Gia a knowing look because she knew that I didn't like to be put on the spot and having my business on front street.

"And he paid for all this so his ass better help us drink it."

"Well, cheers to that." Rae held her shot up and they each took theirs with no problem.

"Gia, I swear the niggas you bring out get finer and finer every night." Ahja had her eyes on someone and so did I.

"Who bitch? Show me."

With their backs turned to us, Ahja and Gia continued their conversation. I couldn't take my eyes off shorty even though I tried to focus my attention elsewhere. It wasn't long before she joined in on their conversation and they started doing their own thing.

Rae had potential. I found myself paying more attention to her every move as she moved around with Gia and Ahja. And call me crazy, but I could still smell her scent, shorty looked good and smelled even better. I loved that about a woman. Personal hygiene was a must. Everything about Rae was on point, her skin was flawless, she had this glow to her, her face was pretty, and she was curvy. She wasn't like the Instagram models, but she was thick, she had enough ass for me.

"Shoot your shot, nigga," Eazy taunted me.

"Chill." I would when the time was right. Gia had already made the introduction and that was all I needed. She'd be hearing from me real soon.

While Gia enjoyed her night with her friends and Eazy joined them, I played the cut just surveying the scene. I may have been the new owner, but I didn't control who came and went so I was just on point. In the midst of all that I kept an eye on Rae. There was a room full of niggas that seemed like they got money too who were surrounding them. I knew Eazy was holding it down but there was but so much he could do because she wasn't mine. I had no rights to that woman. Only Rae didn't seem phased by them at all, and neither did Gia or Ahja. They were so busy in their own world drinking with Eazy that they were barely giving them niggas the time of day. The idea that she wasn't easily phased earned her a few brownie points with me.

KO'RAE

The minutes seemed to drag as I sat behind my desk scrolling through social media. With me working so many hours at the hospital, I was offered three days off, sometimes four depending on the shifts I picked up throughout the week. The perks of working with my best friend was that work never really felt like work. Only today they had moved Ahja to the back because she always had to go above and beyond, and now our manager used her to do everything. My mother would brag about us to her coworkers all the time but Ahja put the icing on the cake with her work ethic. Usually, I matched her energy, it was just today I wasn't feeling it. I was tired. All week Greg had been popping up at my job, calling my phone, calling my mother's phone, just being aggravating as hell like he wasn't the one in the wrong. We were done, I broke it off and I planned on standing on it. He acted like he wasn't the one walking around the club with a bitch that wasn't me. It had been two weeks and I had been ignoring him completely, something he wasn't used to at all. Neither was I, but I was getting used to it. I wasn't doubling back; those days were over.

"Bitch ass nigga," I huffed as I watched Greg's story from my desk.

"What? Why do you look like that?" Ahja asked as she sat beside me closing out her tabs on the computer.

"Greg is corny." I laughed just to keep from aggravating myself any further and handed her my phone so she could see what he posted.

"Rae, fuck Greg. Block him!"

I hadn't brought myself to blocking him on social media. I did block his number because he wouldn't stop calling me, but I just couldn't seem to block his Instagram.

"I don't want to hear shit about Greg tonight," Ahja shot back as she stood up, ready to clock out.

"You won't." I quickly closed the app and gathered my things.

Tonight, we were meeting Gia for drinks after work. Since her birthday we had been trying to hang out more.

"I'm serious, Rae. I'm over the Greg cycle. This time when you say you're done, I hope you mean it."

Ahja walked away, leaving me to my thoughts, and I hoped that I meant it too. I know she thought it was a game, but sometimes my mind and my heart would trick me into believing that he was sorry even when I knew he was lying. If anybody was tired of the back and forth Greg and I commenced, it was Ahja because she was the one who was there for it all.

"We're still meeting Gia tonight, right?" she asked as she strutted back to the front. We were the last two closing up tonight.

"Yes." I was down to go out tonight. It wasn't like I had anything better to do.

"Good, because today drained me. They had me back there working like a slave."

"That's because you need to learn how to say no."

"True, but it helped the day go by faster. I was bored."

"I'm never that bored. Come on, it's six."

"About damn time, it felt like it was 5:59 forever. I hope we make happy hour."

"Girl, every hour is happy hour with Gia. You know she's going to want us to go to her friend's spot."

"Free drinks!" Ahja did a dance as we clocked out, and I closed out my computer before making sure all the copays that I collected today were accounted for before clocking out.

"Your hoe ass is just happy to be seeing Eazy."

"Who said that he's going to be there?"

"Girl, don't play dumb. He's always there."

Ahja tried to play it cool but after that night she gave Eazy her number, he made sure to use it.

"And he sure seems to be a lot of places lately." Just yesterday he was dropping her off food to work and he even picked her up.

"Speaking of, where did y'all go last night?"

"We went out..."

"Hoe."

"I'm not a hoe, we're just hanging out. And you need to stay out my business and focus more on your own, because Brixx—"

"Brixx nothing," I cut her off quickly.

"Rae, don't be like that," she spoke as we walked out to my car.

"I'm not being like anything, and I hope you don't want to go home to change."

"No, because if we go home, you're going to find every excuse in the book to stay home."

"Maybe." I shrugged as I sat down.

"Brixx is feeling you and you know it."

"How would I know that? He seems to be talking to everyone but me about me."

"Girl, have you tried talking to you lately? No. Greg has your head so fucked up that you don't even know how to talk to people anymore. He's probably scared."

"I am not that bad."

"Rae, you are. Eazy just asked me yesterday why you were so mean. I mean, I know you, so I know the real you, but to them you're cold, mean, and you act like you don't want to be bothered."

"Damn," was all I could say because I didn't realize that's how I came off. I didn't mean to.

"Truthfully, I thought all of my Greg drama scared him off," I joked playfully as I waited for Ahja's response. I wasn't too sure how much truth was behind what Ahja was saying so I played it cool.

"Rae, ain't nobody thinking about Greg but you. Trust me, he does not care about Greg. He wants to get to know you."

"Well, if he wants to get to know *me*, what's stopping him? What Nicki say? Like if you see me holler at me, I'm never too ill to say what up, like it's not that serious..." I did my best Nicki impersonation and Ahja burst out laughing because of it.

"Bitch, you need to stay off TikTok. And let's be clear, whenever Brixx is around, you're always so standoffish like you don't want to be bothered. You kind of have to give the man credit though Rae, because even with you acting all stink, he still tries. This Gia calling me now." Ahja placed her phone on speaker once the call connected.

"Thank God y'all are in the car because I'm in Target picking up a bunch of shit that I don't need. How long before y'all get here?"

"Get where?" I asked, even though I already knew where we were going.

"Don't play stupid. You know exactly where we're going." Gia rolled her eyes into the camera as I placed the address in my GPS.

"See you in twenty."

"And Brixx wrote me about you again. If he's there tonight, be nice. Please."

"Whatever." I waved her off because I didn't know that I acted any kind of way that bothered him. The last time we went out I felt a vibe. I felt like there was something there, but with the number of women flocking to him I just let it go. I wasn't up for the challenge.

I will say, he does look good though. He was fine and he knew it. He was cocky, but it was cute, it wasn't arrogant and overbearing. He was just confident in himself, and I liked that. Gia had been in my ear about him since he asked about me the other night and now Ahja was suddenly *Team Brixx*. One thing for certain and two things for sure, Brixx was paid, and no, money was never my motive, but giving up not only my time but my body to a broke nigga was a weak bitch trait. Greg may have been a lot of things, but he wasn't broke.

Brixx had this aura that surrounded him that was almost captivating.

I let Ahja control the music as I drove, and we didn't talk until we pulled up behind Gia and parked.

"Hey G," I greeted Gia, and together the three of us walked toward Allure in our work clothes. Ahja and I in our scrubs and Gia still had her uniform on, everything but her work shirt. Working for School Safety, she couldn't be out in her full uniform when she wasn't on the clock.

Gia made a phone call before we walked inside and like he had been doing whenever she called, Brixx made sure that we were taken care of.

"He's here tonight," she let out, and they both looked at me once we were seated.

"What?"

"Nothing, you better stop playing with that man." Ahja nudged me as she brought my attention to him.

Usually, he wasn't here when we came, at least the last two times he wasn't. Tonight, he was here walking around as if he was a worker and not the boss. Women locked eyes with him and refused to turn away as he swaggered through his establishment with ease. He was dressed in a black Dior hoodie and a pair of jeans that sagged slightly below the band of his Polo boxers. He had Dior sneakers to match his hoodie too. The ice around his neck was almost blinding.

"So much for not being worried about him." Ahja snapped her fingers in my face, breaking me from my train of thought.

"I'm not," I lied and waved her off.

"Yeah right, we can see you sweating him." Gia laughed and they continued to make jokes at my expense.

"Hey G, hey girls, can I get you anything to drink?" KiKi, our server, walked over with a smile and asked. We had only been here a few times but felt familiar with almost everyone in here because Eazy would make sure everyone knew that we were with him when he was here.

"I'll have a Henny colada," I ordered, and Gia and Ahja followed placing their sperate orders.

"Okay, and Brixx told me to bring out some food for y'all, it should be out soon."

"Thank you, and can we get a hookah please? Love 66."

"I got you girl." KiKi walked off toward the bar and my eyes somehow traveled back to where Brixx was standing. The first thing that came to my mind was why was this man single and if he was even really single. I had been around long enough to know that niggas lied. Just because he claimed to be single didn't mean he didn't have someone out there believing they were in a relationship.

Women were walking by him and making their presence known and he didn't turn them away. He was cordial but not friendly. Women with bodies that cost more than my car note and insurance were throwing themselves at him and he would walk away from them with a smile. And here I was sitting here in my scrubs, catching his eye every so often, feeling like a teenage girl. When he smiled at me I tried to look away, but it was too late. He was already on his way over.

"Be nice," Ahja warned, and I waved her off.

"I am nice," I shot back just before he walked up showing all thirty-two teeth.

"How y'all doing tonight?" Brixx spoke as he stood in front of our table.

"Good," I responded like Gia and Ahja, but he only seemed to be looking at me.

"If y'all need anything, just holla. I got y'all," he let us know before turning and walking away.

Brixx kept his distance for the remainder of the night until Eazy walked in demanding that we all take shots. One thing about Eazy, he could drink, and he was making you drink with him. Brixx surprisingly sat and took shots with us unlike the last time we were here. I guess he had time today.

"Ahja, come with me to the bathroom." Gia pulled Ahja away from our table while Eazy was at the bar getting another drink, leaving me and Brixx at the table alone.

"Later, Brixx." A woman with bone-straight red hair and a fat ass waved to Brixx on her way out.

Instead of responding, he smiled and gave her a head nod.

"Rude much?" I joked.

"Oh, you speaking today?" He placed his phone down and looked me in my eyes.

"You need to stop making it seem like I'm this mean person to you. I'm not."

"You could be nicer." He slid into the booth more in an attempt not to yell over the music. Everyone may have been on their way out, but the music was still playing. The scent of his cologne invaded my nostrils instantly.

"What's that you're wearing?" I asked as I tried to control my thoughts as he invaded my personal space. Men flirted with me all the time but there was something about Brixx that made me nervous.

"YSL. You feeling it?"

"It's nice."

"Appreciate it." He smiled, showing off his dimples. His right dimple was way deeper than the left.

"You're welcome." I watched as Ahja and Gia went straight for the bar instead of coming back to the table where I was.

Today was our Friday, so I didn't mind being out past eleven.

This week Ahja and I worked Sunday, Monday, Tuesday, Wednesday, and Thursday, all ten-hour shifts here at the clinic, leaving us to be off Friday, Saturday, Sunday, and Monday for the upcoming week, and I was thrilled.

"So, what's up, you not feeling me?" he asked as he closed the space between us. Brixx was forward, that's for sure.

"Huh?"

"It's all good. You can tell me no, it's a'ight."

"I...I don't know what you mean," I stuttered. This man had me tripping and stumbling over my words.

"I'm feeling you. I'd like to get to know you. I thought it was obvious. I know your girl told you."

"Why couldn't you tell me?" I asked boldly, figuring I'd cut through all the yellow tape.

"Oh, it's like that? Well, I'm telling you now." He smiled.

Brixx had me under pressure and it wasn't often that I'd meet a man and he had me feeling so uneasy. Usually, I was super confident, but Brixx had me questioning a few things. He had me feeling like I had no game.

"I'm not usually this forward but I think that you're beautiful and I'd like to take you out."

"I find that hard to believe."

"Which part?"

If he kept smiling like this my words wouldn't make sense. I was starting to sweat and everything. It had to be the shots taking their course through my body.

Brixx was grilling me, waiting for me to answer, but I couldn't seem to find the words.

"Look, I'm going to Houston for a few days and I heard from a little birdie that you were a big Anthony Davis fan. The Rockets play the Lakers Saturday..."

"In Houston?"

"Yeah," he said it so casually, as if he wasn't asking me to fly to another state for a basketball game.

"Am I wrong? Don't tell me—"

"No, you're right, I love Anthony Davis, but are you asking me to come to Houston for the basketball game?"

"The game and good vibes. I'd love to take you and maybe we can grab something to eat, and I can show you around."

"Are you from Houston?"

"Nah. I have family out there and I spent summers out there, so it's like a second home. One of them at least."

"Oh."

"Can I? I'll pay for your flight and everything..."

I was still stuck on the fact that he put in the work to find out what I liked. I had been dying to see Anthony Davis in person. I thought the closest I would get to that was when the Lakers played the Knicks, but Brixx had other plans.

"I don't know..."

"What's wrong? I'm not no creep ass nigga. I'm solid, you can ask Gia and she'll vouch for me." He smiled at me again, causing me to melt under his gaze.

Now that I thought about it, this had Gia and Ahja written all over it. Just the other day we were talking, and I was telling them how I wanted to go a basketball game, and now here Brixx was offering to take me.

As I sat across from him, I battled with what I would say. Should I go? I mean, I should go, right? It was Anthony Davis, and I knew by the way Brixx carried himself that the seats would be to die for. Even if they weren't, I would just be happy to be there. And who asks someone on a date to another city? A first date at that. I had to go, I needed to see if he could back up all that he was saying. And it wouldn't hurt getting out of NY for a day or two.

"Take my number down and if you want to go, just let me know, a'ight. I'll book your flight, all you have to do is show up."

I handed him my phone so he could save his number. Since Gia's second birthday outing, we talked via Instagram, but it wasn't anything serious. He just reacted to a few things that I posted and we'd have small conversations here and there.

Once he saved his number he stood up and headed toward the back. Fifteen minutes later he was leaving out while I waited for Gia and Ahja to finish their conversation with Eazy at the bar.

"Ready?" I asked them both when they finally came back to the table where I had been sitting by myself since Brixx got up almost an hour ago.

"Yup. Where did Brixx go?"

"He left, I think," I let them know as we made our way to the exit. I wasn't too sure if he had gone home or not, I just know that he walked outside and had yet to return.

When we walked outside Brixx was standing near a Mercedes AMG GLA, the very car that I begged my brother to get me and ended up with a Honda instead.

Instead of going straight to the car, Ahja was off talking to Eazy and Gia was wrapped up in a conversation with a girl from the bar.

"They don't know how to go home either, huh?" Brixx broke the silence that consumed me while I stood patiently waiting for them.

"They don't." I laughed because just from being around Eazy a few times, I could tell that he didn't know when it was time to leave an event either.

"Yo, I meant to press you about not hitting me back either. You too good to hit me back?"

"I thought I did, sorry. You don't have to keep coming at me like that." I felt attacked but not in a harmful way. It was just in a way that I knew he wasn't into letting anything slide.

The last message I remembered getting from him was a response to a story I had posted late last night.

"Nah, I sent you something else. Check your phone." He smiled with so much confidence.

While his tall frame towering over me, I reached into my bag to retrieve my phone and check our DMs while I overheard Ahja and Eazy deep in conversation. Gia had to be on the phone with Kash, because all they did was argue.

"You must think that you're some type of comedian." My words weren't as pleasant as the smile on my face.

"It's funny though, right? I see you smiling."

"If it's not directed, I don't respect it," I joked.

"It's directed, you just like playing games. I told you what was up with me already. The ball is in your court now, love."

"Wait, why is it on me?"

"Because you didn't say that you'd come with me to Houston. Unless you want me to book your flight right now?" He shrugged casually as he moved his hands from his pockets to his beard.

"Houston? Like Texas, are you for r—"

"Nah like—"

"Don't be a smart ass." I gave him a look and rolled my eyes at his attempt to come for me.

"I'm just messing with you. I'd really like for you to come out there though. We can go to the game and I'll show you around. We can do whatever you want. I have some business to handle out there tomorrow. I don't know what your work schedule is like, but I could fly you out there the day after tomorrow. The game is on Saturday..." Brixx was almost pleading with his eyes and under his gaze I felt heat.

"Just like that, huh?"

"It's nothing to it, trust me. I won't press you about it, but I'll be waiting on that text. A'ight? I want you to come, that's if you have the time for me and if you done messing with soft ass niggas who don't appreciate what they have right in front of them."

"Mm, okay." My voice trailed off as I watched him walk away as he back pedaled to his car. His skin was almost glowing under the night sky.

"That's my bitch!" Ahja walked up just as Eazy was making his way to Brixx's car.

"You need to stop."

She waved me off.

"No girl, you need to stop fronting. Don't forget that I know you, like really know you better than you know yourself. You like him."

"He's cool…"

"Cool my ass. Stop being so coy and for sure stop worrying about what you think other people think, because fuck them! You are grown Rae and there's a man as fine as he is who is interested in you and wants to spend time and get to know you. I want you to go for it. You should want to go for it."

"He wants me to fly to Houston Saturday for the Lakers game."

"Well I'll be damned. Go head Brixx, do yo' shit."

"Y'all, should I go on this date? I mean, damn, who does shit like this?"

"Niggas with money, Rae. It's about time you come up off that low down, dirty dick, conniving, cheap ass nigga. You should go, and plus, the way that nigga walks around, I know he got good dick."

"Dick that'll fuck my life up, I bet," I joked, because Brixx did have that aura about him.

"Whew, I'm jealous. So, what are you going to wear to the game?" she asked me as we made our way to my car where Gia was already standing.

"I mean, I've been looking for the right time to wear my Givenchy boots."

"Yasss, bitch. Greg who?"

I could honestly say that I hadn't thought about Greg all night. I wasn't sure if it was because Ahja was constantly screaming fuck him or was it because Brixx seemed to occupy space in my mind tonight.

"Is it wrong that I'm afraid of how I could possibly lose myself in another nigga, especially in someone like Brixx?"

"It's not wrong, but your tender-hearted ass needs to learn how to have some fun. You won't. You're dating, have fun," Gia added in our conversation as if she didn't miss a beat.

GAME NIGHT

When I landed last night Brixx picked me up from the airport and took me to get something to eat before taking me back to my room where we stayed up all night just talking. So far Brixx had been surprising me left and right. Here I was thinking he was just like every other nigga, and he was far from it.

"You look beautiful," Brixx complimented me as he held my hand tightly, leading me to his car. This man rented a Maserati and I had never seen one up close and personal before. I mean, my brother rented exotic foreign cars all the time, but the Maserati wasn't one of them, so this was a first for me. This entire experience was a first for me. I held my roses in one hand and slid in the passenger seat as he held the door open for me.

A few moments ago, Brixx stood on the other side of my room door with a dozen long-stem roses. My heart was beating out of my chest as we walked down the long hallway to the elevator. I was so nervous that even the palms of my hands were sweating.

"I love these." I smiled as he pulled off and I admired the red roses.

I spent over an hour getting dressed with Ahja on FaceTime. I wanted to look cute but I also wanted to be comfortable. I decided to wear my black bodysuit, one of many that I had from Zara, and Ahja coached me into wearing a black pleated skirt with my Givenchy boots. I topped off my outfit with my Chanel Black Quilted Medium Boy Bag. My makeup appointment was courtesy of Gia. She found me an MUA out here and booked my appointment. My hair was re-done in small knotless braids that I had parted to the side. And all my jewelry was courtesy of Nine. My brother bought me diamond earrings and a chain a year ago.

"How was your day?"

"It was good, and thank you for earlier."

"You're welcome. Thank you for being patient."

Because Brixx was busy with a meeting, he sent me money to

go shopping earlier and to explore a little on my own while he handled his business. At first, I was hesitant to accept his money or even go out on my own, but once he assured me that he'd be close, I took the liberty of doing some sightseeing and light shopping at the mall while on FaceTime with Ahja the entire time. I even picked him up something.

"I know I promised you that I'd show you around, but m—"

"You don't have to explain, it's okay. I enjoyed my day."

"I know, but I still want to make it up to you. I made sure that my schedule was clear for tomorrow, so I'm all yours."

"But my flight is tomorrow."

"Arrangements can be made as long as you want them to be."

"Okay."

When we arrived at the arena I was impressed. Brixx rode through all the traffic and commotion with ease, following the signs that led to reserved VIP parking.

VIP?

The parking lot was lined with top-of-the-line cars just like his.

"Thank you." I thanked him as he held the door opened for me and helped me out the car. Brixx had been the perfect gentleman all night, something I had yet to experience.

As we walked through the arena, I wasn't sure what to expect so when he led me courtside, I was stunned. As we moved in the opposite direction of the crowd on our way to our seats, Brixx held my hand tightly and escorted me the entire way.

I remembered my brother's voice in this moment and him telling me that a real man will go the extra mile for you. He will wine and dine you with no regard to the expense too, and that's how you'll know if he's worth a second date. Nine was always dropping little jewels whenever he was around.

"This is... I don't even know what to say." I smiled as he allowed me to sit down before he sat beside me.

"I knew I had to come correct. How am I doing so far?" He smiled.

"Okay," I spoke modestly, already knowing that I was loving every second of this experience. Since I landed, Brixx had been sure to make sure that I was comfortable.

"Just okay, I respect it. I have to come harder." He seemed to be in deep thought, and I found it cute.

"I'm just playing. You're doing amazing, I'm having a great time."

I felt like a celebrity sitting front row.

There were so many people in attendance and here I was sitting courtside with this fine ass nigga. I had never been to a Knicks game, and I've lived in New York my entire life, so for my first game to be in another city spoke volumes. I had voiced to Greg many times how badly I wanted to go to a game and as much as he entertained the idea, he never jumped at the chance to take me. Whereas with the repost of a meme on IG, I found myself sitting courtside with a man I had just met and barely knew anything about.

What we saw on TV was nothing compared to the vibe in the arena. The music was loud, the crowd was live, and the players were up close and personal. There were plenty of celebrities in attendance and I had been scanning the crowd since I sat down.

"You good?" Brixx looked over at me to check on me.

"Yes. In awe, but I'm fine."

"You look it too," he complimented me as he had been doing since he picked me up from the hotel.

"Thank you." I had been blushing all night. Under his stare I felt hot yet safe.

As the players dribbled up and down the court, I sat back in amazement with my head going left to right in an attempt to keep up with each play. I loved the energy Brixx had throughout the game. I was a big fan of basketball, and he matched my energy. We cheered together, booed together, and talked shit the entire game.

Brixx held great conversation. On the ride here we talked, and I could sense that there was more to him than what the eyes could see. I liked my men thugged out but intelligent too.

After the game Brixx led me back to the VIP parking area where we agreed to go for drinks after. He said he knew a place where the courtside ticket holders went after the game, and I was looking forward to it. I was having such a good time I didn't care where we went. I wasn't ready for our night to end.

"So, Brixx, what are you into?" I asked as we sat at the bar and I sipped on my lemon drop.

"A little bit of everything to be honest, but eventually I'm looking to own a chain of night clubs and lounges in different cities."

"Hmm, so you must love the night life?"

"I do. I spent most of my nights on the block hustling and I even did a little party promoting back in the day. I know how it might seem, but I'm really just trying to build generational wealth off some street money."

"Well, kudos to you." I held my glass to his.

"What about you?"

"I work. I work a lot, but my days off are good, so I guess it pays off."

"Where you work? I peeped you in scrubs the other night."

"I work in the hospital at the clinic. I went to school to be a nurse but then my brother went to jail, and I stopped paying my tuition. It's a long story but I love my job, even when they piss me off. I just love helping people."

"That's what's up."

We sat in silence for a moment before Brixx boldly stood up and pulled me with him as a slow jam played.

"What are you doing?"

"Can I have this dance?" he asked as he held my hand in his, using it to pull my body closer to him.

"Yes."

"I like you and that's different for me," he explained, and I just stood there moving my body back and forth to the beat of the music.

"You're pretty cool too," I joked, not really knowing what else to say. For some reason, Brixx made me nervous.

"I'm just pretty cool, huh?"

"Yup." I looked Brixx in his eyes, almost getting lost in them.

No words were spoken, only the music serenaded our ears before his lips came crashing down on mine. And his big, strong hands traveled to my back, making his way to my ass. Brixx grabbed a handful of my ass and stuck his tongue in my mouth.

"Mmmmm," I moaned as I felt a wave of heat rush my body and his lips kissed my neck. As my body rocked back and forth, Brixx held me as if we were the only ones here.

"I'm so sorry to interrupt, but we're closing." An older white man came and tapped Brixx on his shoulder, pulling us from our little bubble of ecstasy.

I quickly snapped back into reality and went to finish my drink while Brixx closed out our tab. I was three lemon drops in and he was on his fourth shot of tequila.

On our way out, Brixx gave me this look that said, "I want to fuck," but I could tell that he was trying to keep it PG. I was just going with the flow. I had never felt this comfortable with a man before. Maybe it was the liquor, but the thought of fucking this fine ass nigga back at the hotel didn't sound too bad.

With our hands intertwined, Brixx led the way to his car, continuing to be the perfect gentleman.

"Thank you." I thanked him for opening the passenger door for me.

"You're welcome, beautiful." I looked up at him in awe because with ease he had made me comfortable to walk hand in hand with him in public.

"I hope you not just using a nigga to get your mind off that other nigga."

"What nigga?" I smirked slyly, and he nodded.

Brixx bit down on his bottom lip and I could only imagine where his head was at. There was lust in his eyes as I matched his gaze. My eyes were filled with lust and I wondered if he saw it and just chose to ignore it or just missed it altogether.

"You deserve better."

"Brixx, I don't want to talk about him."

"I don't want to talk about the nigga either, but I just wanted you to hear it from me. I can tell that the nigga hurt you, I see it all in your face. And I just know that you deserve better than that. You too smart, too beautiful, and have too much going for yourself to deal with a weak nigga and to let him treat you so poorly. Feel me?"

He stepped back a few inches and from the look on his face, I could tell that he was serious.

"He doesn't make me happy, and I know I deserve better but I'm here with you and he's the last person on my mind. I'm not that girl, if I even felt like I wanted to salvage an ounce of what I had with him, I wouldn't be here. That would not only be disrespectful to you but myself."

Silence consumed us for a moment.

Instead of a verbal response, he nodded and that was the end of that conversation. The last thing I wanted to do was spend the rest of our night speaking on my ex.

I was left looking at his retreating back as he made his way around the car to the driver's side. Had Ahja been here, she would have been telling me to pick up my jaw with the way I was sitting here waiting for him to get in the car.

A part of me could tell that Brixx was trying to make space and time for me in his life and in the process of that, he wanted to know if I was doing the same. And from the way his phone was blowing up all day and he was rearranging meetings and ignoring calls, I could tell that he was making the time we spent together a priority.

"I want to do more of this if you let me."

"I'd like that."

"I know you're taking a chance fucking with me, but I can almost guarantee that you'll enjoy it."

"That's a pretty big statement…"

"I know. And I plan to stand on it too." He was looking at me so intensely that I prayed he was serious.

I had dealt with my fair share of men in my life, thugs, scammers, working men, but Brixx was already showing me that he was on a whole other level. He was the first man that intimidated me in a way. It wasn't a feeling of fear that resided in me either, it just wasn't one of comfortability. It was one that I looked forward to exploring.

Later that night, I laid in my hotel room alone after a hot shower with the biggest smile. I had just gotten off FaceTime with Gia and Ahja, filling them in on my date, and now I was ready to call it a night. After fighting it for the sake of conversation with my girls, sleep finally came over me and I was out like a light.

Knock…knock…

Two light taps later turned into three harder taps.

Knock…knock…knock…

Stirring in my sleep, I instantly reached for my phone to check the time and was met by a missed call and a message from Brixx.

Good morning beautiful, I figured I'd let you sleep in. Hit me when you wake up.

The message and the missed call were time stamped for eleven a.m. and it was now going on twelve thirty. Thinking he was who was at my door, I ran to the bathroom to freshen up.

Knock…knock…knock…knock…

With the biggest smile, I looked myself over in the mirror as I brushed my teeth and washed my face.

"I'm cominggg," I sang as I applied lotion to my hands and opened the door in a robe and fresh face.

"Mrs. Sanders, these are for you." The man on the other side of the door was pleasant but he wasn't Brixx. Disappointment began to settle in unwillingly for a moment, until I laid my eyes on the dozen roses the man held in his arms for me.

"Oh, thank you." I smiled, feeling full inside as I accepted the flowers and prepared to close the door.

"Oh, ma'am, there are plenty more." It wasn't until now that I peered into the dimly lit hallway and noticed three carts full of flowers.

"Oh my god," I gasped in awe. "Is there a card?"

"Yes, here it is." The gentleman handed me the pink and white card as I stood admiring the beautiful flower arrangements. Roses were my favorite. There was an assortment of colors, but the red and yellow rose compositions were my favorite. I had never seen so many flowers before, all for me at that.

I hope you slept well, be ready for lunch at three.

-BRIXX

"Here's another." The man handed me two more cards as I stood there overwhelmed.

Thank you for making time for me. Giving a nigga a chance to get to know you.

The third card was cute, it read:

Out of body, that's just how I feel when I'm around ya.
Last night we didn't say it but, I know we both were thinking it.
Why second guess what feels right?
I should've said.. I should've did.. but I didn't.
Just say the word and I'm coming for ya.
Whenever you need me, wherever you want me, I'm there for ya.

I re-read the third card with a smile as he put his own twist on "Teenage Fever" by Drake. I didn't take Brixx for the romantic type, yet here I was standing in a room full of flowers with three cards.

Snapping a quick picture, I sent a photo of my room to the girls in our group chat. It was after twelve thirty here so that meant in New York it was going on two o'clock. Gia and Ahja responded within minutes.

GIA: *Aww Rae, that nigga not playing 'bout you, I love that for you!*

AHJA: *That's how real niggas come? I need me one.*

GIA: *Brixx finna have Rae's ass so far gone and I'm here for it.*

AHJA: *Let me go back to sleep and see if I wake up to roses too.*

Ahja and Gia went on for a good twenty minutes, just carrying on. I had never seen so many flowers in one space in my life, all for me. I felt good.

After basking in the moment for another half hour of being on the phone with Ahja, I checked the time and knew I needed to get ready. It was going on one thirty in the afternoon and Brixx wanted me ready at three. What I've realized over the last two days was how punctual he was. If he said three then he meant three, not three thirty or even 3:01.

After my shower I tore through my suitcase looking for something to wear. The plan was for us to go to the game and the game only. Good thing I was quick on my feet and packed an array of outfits. One of the perks of being indecisive. Aside from my Shark Boots, I packed my favorite pair of Rick Owens, my Chanel sneakers, and even my off-white Muslin 5's. I had outfits that could go with each sneaker. With Brixx being so laid back, I got ready with ease. I wasn't questioning what I wore just what I wanted to put on. I was looking forward to spending time with him. The two of us just sitting down and spending time together was enough.

Standing in front of the hotel mirror, I laid my edges and placed my diamond halo stud earrings in. It was nearing two forty-five and I was shocked that I was dressed and ready. I decided to wear my Chanel sneakers, Amiri jeans, and a white fitted t-shirt from my fave, Zara. Casual but cute is what I was going for and was what I was giving. I sprayed my Marc Jacobs perfume and waited for the text or call to come down.

BRIXX

SHORTY KNOWS THAT I'M THE BEST SHE
NEVER HAD

"You are just full of surprises." I watched Rae as she walked out the lobby with the biggest smile.

With one single rose, I stood outside the car waiting to greet her as she exited the hotel lobby. I could admit shorty had me doing things I've never done before. The date, the game, the kiss, the roses... the whole nine was not me, it wasn't my lane.

"Hi..."

"What up? You slept good?" I handed her the rose trying to keep it G, but she made me feel comfortable enough to let my guard down.

"I did."

With my arms opened, I offered her a hug and she accepted. I liked that she smelled fresh whenever I was around her and that she was always smiling. I liked the way she looked up at me with her brown eyes searching my soul. I liked the way her lips felt when I kissed her, and I wasn't that nigga. It wasn't like me to go around kissing females so freely. With Rae though, just being in her presence was different. She was a force, she took up space, and I liked that. From the day that I met her, Rae caught my attention.

Rae had the credentials of the woman my niggas bragged

about when they saw her. She was one of the ones niggas spoke about when they were thinking of settling down and having something real or even remotely close to it.

I craved intimacy. As a man, most niggas liked to front like it wasn't something they wanted. I wanted it, only with the right person. Was Rae the *right* person for me? That I didn't know just yet, but I was for damn sure going to explore and find out. I enjoyed spending time with her, talking to her, joking with her, and just being in her space. Her honesty and openness proved to me how soft she was. She was soft in the most respectful and healthiest way possible. Because even with her going through what she was going through, she was still willing to put herself out there. I respected that. I appreciated her giving a nigga like me a chance in the first place. Niggas like me didn't get the girl, we got the *money*.

"Thank you for my flowers. What am I supposed to do with all of them? My room is full of roses and I have a flight for the morning," she asked me as I handed her the single rose and pressed my lips against hers lightly.

"Whatever you want to do with them. I'll send you more." I walked around the car to open the door for her and appreciated her scent. Rae was beautiful, she looked angelic-like. It made me feel good that she took the time to get herself together each time I saw her. Even on some chill shit, she was still fly.

"Oh, it's just that easy?"

"It's whatever you want it to be. It's *your* world." The smile I offered her had her smiling back at me.

"What?" she questioned me, and I knew exactly why. I had my eyes trained on her as I started the car.

"Don't look at me like that..."

It was hard to believe that she was done with her ex just like that. Or if that nigga was even her ex and she was just here with me to get the nigga jealous. She only spoke briefly about her situation, and I didn't push. I wanted her to be comfortable and I truly didn't give a fuck about it. That nigga was old news, yesterday's paper. I didn't do too much digging and I prayed he didn't have a hold on her, because I wanted her. I wanted her to be mine and I wasn't looking to share with nan nigga.

"I like looking at you. You're beautiful."

"Thank you." She blushed as I drove to The Breakfast Klub, a spot I hit up every time I came to Houston.

"You're welcome."

"Brixx, I don't know how to thank you. I really enjoyed myself this weekend. You've been spoiling me from the minute I landed."

I planned on spoiling her some more. Little did she know, this was just the beginning. I was going to make sure that she was good, she deserved it. Rae was raw, she was genuine, and you didn't come by females like that often.

"If I have my way, I plan on spoiling you some more."

"Oh, so you plan on sticking around?" she asked innocently with a hint of laughter in a possible attempt to keep the conversation light.

I wouldn't even front, it made me feel good that she was on the same page as me. We both seemed to want to spend more time together. Even though things were just starting out with us, Rae was liable to take a nigga out the game for good.

"That's the plan. If you'd allow me."

We pulled up to The Breakfast Klub where the line was almost out the door.

"You've been the perfect gentleman. I can get used to this," she let me know with a smile as I held the car door open for her and helped her out the car.

"I am a gentleman, don't sound so surprised." I kept my hand in hers as we walked to the entrance together.

"I am. Seriously, for starters, you flew me out here, you took me on the one date that I had been dying to go on for months, and you've treated me like a total princess the entire time..."

"I'm not no creep ass nigga, Rae. I don't expect anything from you in return..."

"That's not what I was getting at, Sir. It's just a lot to take in and to be honest, it wasn't something that I expected from you..."

Rae did have me out of my element and on my gentleman shit. There wasn't a woman alive who can say that they received the same treatment as Rae, not even Neesha. She let me fuck the first night and I never had to do much of anything for her but give her some money here and there. This was all new to me, but I planned on showing Rae a different side to me and giving her the best.

"Who don't you know?" Rae shook her head as I dapped up the hostess and bypassed the long line.

"I know a few people," I joked as I led her to the back where my usual table was located.

"Do you own this place as well?"

"Nah, I wish. Maybe one day I'll spin the block for it if the owner is ever looking to sell or some shit."

"You make the impossible seem possible."

I smiled at that. No one had said anything like that to me before. Most women would just go with the flow and watch a nigga's pockets. My money was always at the forefront of their minds, but with Rae it was different. I mean, I know she thought about it, but it's the way she presented it that set her apart from everyone else. I was rich, I was a wealthy nigga, but my money didn't define who I was as a man.

"Do I really?"

"Yes. I mean, it's every dope boys dream to make it out and live the life of luxury. And there aren't many that get to accomplish that. You should be proud of yourself."

Rae spoke to me like I was human, not like I was a meal ticket or like she was just feeding a nigga a bunch of lies and bullshit. Her delivery seemed sincere and genuine.

"I appreciate that." I tried to keep the big ass smile that was threating to spread across my face under wraps, but it wasn't even worth it.

"No problem, men deserve their flowers too. What you're

doing, what you've done shouldn't go unnoticed. I love that you didn't allow the hype of the streets to define you or even break you."

"What you know about the streets?"

"I'm from Marcy, I know a lot about the streets. Plus, both my older brother and father were in the streets, so I was exposed to a lot."

I let out a stiff chuckle at her reference to being from Marcy.

"What?" she asked.

"Nothing." I shook my head and smiled.

Rae made me motivated to continue to do more, to continue to wow her. It felt good that she saw a nigga and appreciated what I had going for myself.

We continued to talk and placed our orders in the meantime. I knew I was stuck on her because of the daze she had me in while I sat just listening to her talk.

After sitting across from her and really just talking and listening, I was sure that I was feeling her. My mind wasn't on anything and anyone but her as I sat across from her. Rae needed reassurance and I was the perfect nigga to give it to her. I set the bar high by fucking with her because I didn't want her to ever get the feeling that I wasn't feeling her, because I was. Who I was in the streets wasn't the same man that was sitting across from her. It took me trial and error to get here and to be honest, I had fumbled a lot. I even mishandled and misused plenty of women who probably truly cared about me. I just wasn't ready to receive it back then, I had a lot of growing to do.

"Brixx, be honest, what made you want to ask me out?"

"Damn... to be real, it was your smile and the way that you handled yourself. I'm not going to front, I was tight that night of Gia's birthday when you popped on ol' boy..."

"Here we go... Listen, I'd rather you get it off your chest now so we can just move past it."

"Nah, hear me out. I was only tight because I had just mustered up the courage to walk over to you and introduce myself before you started spazzing. But even after all that, I still wanted to get to know you so I hit Gia up to see if she could put me on. Once we got to talking, I was able to get a glimpse of how cool you actually were. On top of that, Gia spoke highly of you and she didn't do that often about other females, so off rip I was intrigued. I don't know if I'm even answering your question properly, but you just being who you are made me want to pursue you."

"So you asked her about other females?"

"Huh?"

"Yeah..." She laughed, knowing that she caught me up, but didn't trip over it. I fucked with that.

I was as open as I could have been in this moment. And this was a moment that Rae showed me once again why she was nothing like other women. She was more concerned about me and how I thought and felt as opposed to my bag. The way she smiled after I spoke let me know that she was satisfied with my answer.

After brunch, we rode around the city, and I showed Rae my version of Houston. Houston was like my second home and before we headed back to the hotel, we stopped for ice cream at Honeychild's Sweet Creams, a spot that she found on TikTok and just had to have.

"Will that be all?" the woman at the register asked, and I nodded.

"Yes. And I'm paying." Rae slipped in front of me and handed the cashier two twenty-dollar bills against my will, and all I could do was let her be.

Everything was going better than expected and I knew it was going to be hard for me to let her go back to her life back in the city without me in it. I almost wanted to cancel our flights and stay another day just because I wasn't ready to let her leave just yet. But there was this gut feeling I got that this wasn't going to be the last that I saw of her. Our time together out here gave me more than enough time to come to the conclusion that I wanted her, and I usually always got what I wanted.

BACK IN THE CITY

I walked through LaGuardia Airport with Rae, grateful. I had just spent the best three days with her, and I wasn't happy that she was leaving me.

"Brixx, I had such a good time. Thank you." Rae stood in front of me with her luggage beside her while we waited for Ahja to pull up and pick her up.

"You're welcome, ma. Hit me when you get home, alright?"

"Okay." She smiled and looked up at me, confusing the hell out of me. On one hand, I wanted to grab her hand and take her with me, and on the other, I knew that there was business I needed to take care of first that needed my full attention uptown.

"Hey Brixx," Ahja spoke once she rolled the window down.

"What up Ahja, you good?"

"Yes, did you two have fun?"

"I'll let your girl tell you all about it. Rae, come here." I stopped her from placing her bags in the trunk and did it for her. When I was done, I pulled her close to me and hugged her tightly.

"Will I see you later?" she asked with a fake pout that had me ready to cancel all my plans.

"For sure. I'll hit you once I make it to the crib."

"Mmhmm."

"You got my word."

"Is it crazy that I feel like I'm about to miss you?"

"Nah, if you didn't miss a nigga even just a little, I'd be feeling some type of way. Once I finish uptown, I'll check in."

"Okay. Later." She offered me the prettiest smile and a hug. I couldn't resist her or the urge to kiss her, so I did.

"Hello," I answered my ringing phone as I slid into the Uber Black car moments after Rae and Ahja pulled off.

"Yo, I handled that uptown situation already. You don't have to go up there."

"You sure?"

"Yeah, it's all good. How was the trip?"

"It was cool." I caught myself smiling just at the thought of Rae.

"Alright then. Hit me when you get to the crib."

"Yo, my man," I called out to the driver and explained to him that I no longer needed to go to the address I had initially requested. I offered him cash to take me home without the hassle of me requesting a new ride.

"Good looking." I thanked him and handed him the hundred-dollar bill that I had for him once we pulled up to my crib.

"Yo, I'm about to hit the mall. You sliding with me?"

"Let me go drop this money off to Ahja and I'll be over that way in a minute."

"I'll meet you over there."

Any reason to see Rae was a good enough reason for me. I didn't mind making that drive for her.

"You miss her already, nigga?"

"I'll see you in a minute." I was trying to play it cool because I knew that if I answered any other way, Eazy would drag it. With Eazy it was like having that annoying little brother that wanted to be in everything that you were in.

"Don't front, nigga. You're feeling her. Nigga always trying to be too cool for school, but Rae might be just what you need."

I could hear the laughter in his voice and I knew this wasn't the last that I was going to hear of it.

"You gotta chill, my nigga."

"I'm just saying, that's family now. Any female that can get you to spend more than just a few hours with them is different. You don't even take bitches on dates, yet you flew Rae out when you had a bunch of shit on your plate. Don't forget that I know you, nigga."

For once, Eazy was making sense. He had a point, but there was no way in hell that I was about to tell him he was right.

"Slow your roll and stay out my business."

"What I'm trying to say is you deserve it. You deserve her if she's who—"

"Yo, I'm going to hit you when I'm on my way over there." I had to stop Eazy before he got too ahead of himself.

"You a funny nigga. You need to enjoy the moment and have some fun," he spoke his peace before he hung up, because he just had to have the last word.

I hopped in a quick shower, threw on one of my Essentials sweatsuits and my off-white Muslin 5's, then grabbed some money and my wallet. I didn't put on any jewelry, aside from my diamond earrings. I was chilling and we were just running to the mall. I was transitioning to my grown man shit, real boss shit. I had a few tailored suits I was waiting to pick up. I wasn't sagging my jeans like the rest of these little niggas out here in dingy clothes. I took my clothes to the cleaners and if it wasn't a regular throw-on sweatsuit, I barely wore my clothes more than once. Since the year started, I had been leaving that corner boy mindset behind and leveling up to a businessman.

When I pulled up on Eazy he was just leaving out of Ahja's building. I peeped his car parked across the street and him walking in the opposite direction.

"What up." Eazy dapped me when he slid into the passenger seat of my truck and we made our way to the mall.

I made my rounds through Prada, Loui, Gucci, Nordstrom, and Zara. Bottega and Balenciaga were two brands that I was on heavy right now. Prada had just dropped some heat too. The new colorways for their Americas Cup sneakers were fire, so I copped two pair.

"You can never come here and just chill." Eazy shook his head as he watched me load all my bags in the back of my truck.

"When I die, I can't take it with me, so why not blow a bag on myself every now and then. I work hard for mine, I might as well ball out."

"Yo, about that uptown situation. I went up there because I know the lane you're switching to now and I respect it. The street shit just isn't you anymore and I know that."

"It's not *us* anymore. We've made more than enough money out here. It's time to let other niggas eat and have their way. I'm ready to give it all up, my nigga."

"I know. I'm right there with you. I just need to find my lane."

"I hear you." It wouldn't do me or Eazy any good if I pushed him to get out before he was ready to. Once I hit that milli mark last year, I ran it up and doubled it. I saw more money off the streets this last year than I did on the streets all those years prior. It was time for me to focus on legal shit and I wanted Eazy to reap the benefits as well.

Eazy was a street nigga to the core. He was in the streets heavy way before we met at sixteen and I didn't fault him for it, he was just a product of his environment. As was I. The streets weren't kind to him. Eazy had been through some things, but I knew once he was ready to get out he'd leave on his own terms, and I'd be there waiting for him.

"I'm dead ass, I know I be on some wild shit, but a nigga is ready to hang it up. These streets don't love nobody. And after I went uptown to chop it up with Dread, I realized that niggas are hungry. I just want to make sure I secure that pipeline for niggas before I part ways."

Eazy was one selfless nigga. That I could say about him and mean it. He'd give a nigga the shirt off his back if they needed it. Little did he know, I had given him 50 percent ownership of the lounge because I knew he needed a start. He needed to have a safe place to clean his dirty money.

"Yo, what's up with you and Ahja?"

"Nun nigga, we're just chilling. Don't get me wrong, I shot my shot, but Ahja is not one of them. She knew a nigga was on bullshit the moment I approached her." He shook his head in disappointment, and I knew he wasn't used to being turned down by a female.

"She shot your ass down?"

"Respectfully." Eazy laughed as he shook his head. "It's cool though, I know she's feeling me, but she's just scared to admit it because of the nigga I am."

"She knows that you're a hoe and she don't want nothing to do with that messy shit."

"I'm young, I'm just having fun. And I know she's been through some things. And forcing her to fuck with me right now would just add on to that hurt. I'm not trying to be that nigga."

"Ahja got your ass thinking clearly for once. She might be the one to sit your ass down."

"Maybe. I'm not against it. I fuck with her. She's mad cool, we be chopping it up about everything."

"I know you fuck with her if you're dropping money off to her."

"She's just holding some cash for me. You know I don't leave money at the crib."

"Hopefully she can slow your ass down. You can't be out here fucking every bitch you see."

"That's true, we didn't even fuck yet and you would think that I would be out here fucking around, but I haven't been. Nigga, I've been under Ahja's ass so much my hoes cut me off."

I chopped it up with Eazy while we passed a blunt back and forth before pulling out the parking lot to the mall.

Rae and Ahja were two black women who had their shit together, and it felt good to sit here while my nigga bragged about them.

What up beautiful, just checking in. You good?

Hey, I'm fine, hungry.

What you want to eat? I'll come pick you and Ahja up right now.

Aren't you across town?

I'll be there soon, a'ight?

Okay, see you soon.

"Yo, you moved all that weight out your spot though, right?"

"Come on my nigga, you know I did. I wouldn't leave that shit in the crib. I took it uptown with me."

"Bet. We don't need niggas knowing we have that much work anyway. You're the only nigga that knows how much work we have coming in this month."

"I hope you're not questioning my loyalty."

"Never that. I'm just showing you mine. You're my brother, I eat, you eat."

Eazy was my brother, and I was my brother's keeper.

I learned early on that you couldn't put your trust in just any nigga. Snakes came a dime a dozen in all shapes and sizes.

If everything worked out for us with this shipment, we would be bringing in close to two hundred twenty-two million dollars easily, and I was leaving the game after that. My time was up, so it was time to let other niggas be on top and eat.

Within the hour we were pulling up to Ahja's building and Rae was the first to come out. Looking her over, I noticed that she had changed her clothes and we were almost matching.

"You trying to be like me?" I rolled down my window to speak to her.

"No, you're trying to be like me." She didn't even know what I was talking about, yet she was popping her shit.

Even in a sweatsuit and sneakers Rae still had my attention. Just like the first time I laid eyes on her, my heart started beating funny, doing things I had never felt before. It was all so crazy to me because I hadn't felt this way in a long time. The last female that had me feeling beside myself was a fraud. That bitch was a con artist, and every time I looked into Rae's eyes I was searching for some truth, some honesty. I was hoping that I could tell if she was real or not by looking into her eyes. When I looked into her eyes though, I saw hope. And as I got to know her more, I realized that Rae wasn't anything like Neesha's ass. She was different, not thirsty, not money hungry, and she actually had something going for herself.

"I didn't even know you had these." She rolled her eyes once she peeked into the car to see what I was talking about.

"I have everything."

"I bet you do. How are we supposed to fit in here with all your bags in here?" she questioned, and I didn't even think about that.

"It's all good, I'll drive, and Ahja can ride with me."

I nodded and Eazy hopped out the car and met Ahja on the curb since his car was parked across the street.

"So, you missed me that much, huh?" Rae asked as she slid into the passenger seat.

"I did. I told you that I'd see you later."

"You did." She smiled as I pulled off behind Eazy.

"I'm a man of my word. What are you in the mood to eat?"

"Hmm, I don't know, something, anything."

"You ever been to Dive Bar?"

"Yes. We went for Ahja's birthday last year. I had their steak and fries I think. I could go for that."

"Bet."

On the ride there, we spoke casually about the trip and I let her control the aux. I thought she was going to go R&B crazy but she had a solid playlist.

When we pulled up, I opened the door for her and watched her ass jiggled in her tight sweats as we walked from the car to the entrance.

God, please let this woman be who I think she is. I know I'm trying to fill this void in my heart aimlessly, but this shit just feels right.

If Rae was my second chance at love after Neesha, then I was going for it. I know it was soon, but it was one of those things, if you know you know.

While we stood outside waiting to be serviced, Rae stood in front of me, leaving no space between us. Since Houston I contemplated my next move. I knew she felt my dick rising in my sweats as her ass backed up into me discreetly. From the outside looking in the act seemed so innocent, yet it was criminal what she was doing to me. I was dancing with respect and just saying fuck it right now. I respected her and I wanted to make sure that nigga was fully out of her system before we took it there. The last thing I wanted was for her to regret it, that would crush a nigga. When she grabbed my hand as it rested beside me and squeezed it tightly, I knew she felt me, all eight and a half inches of me.

All I wanted to do was ease her pain and eventually take it all away. I wanted to show Rae that I could be the nigga she not only wanted but needed. I wanted to show her better, the better I knew she deserved. I wanted to be in love again, healthy love though, not none of that toxic shit that seemed to be on sale out here. Everything I wanted could have possibly been right in front of me if I played my cards right and she was who I thought she was. The last thing I wanted was to put myself out there with someone who was still on the fence about a no-good ass nigga. Nah, I deserved better than that.

"Thank you for taking me to get something to eat." Rae thanked me on the walk back to the car. The four of us sat down to eat and the girls enjoyed hookah at their leisure.

"You're welcome."

"You seem too good to be true, Brixx." She laughed nervously as I stood with the door open for her.

"I'm just a regular nigga."

"Are you sure? Let me see." She pulled me closer to her as she attempted to examine me.

"What you think?" I asked, playing into whatever game she was playing.

"Hmm, definitely not regular." She ran her hand down my chest and stopped at my waistline with a devious smile plastered on her face.

"I should be the one asking you if you're real. No cap, a nigga has a horrible track record with females. You're the one who seems too good to be true."

"Who me? Oh, baby, not with the drama I have going on around me."

"You mean that bitch ass nigga?"

"Brixx..."

"What? I just call 'em how I see 'em." I shrugged, not really giving a fuck about dude to begin with.

"Okay, we don't have to talk about him."

"We don't, I'm just keeping it real. As a man, he should have done better. You should've never been in a situation where you were compromised like that because a nigga was out here moving foul. That's some lil' boy shit."

"It is..." Her voice trailed off and I could tell that what I said had her in deep thought. "The last thing I want to be talking about while I'm with you is my ex, it's depressing and draining."

She put her head down and I instantly lifted it back up gently.

"Don't do that." I forced her to pick her head up and appreciated the beautiful woman before me.

"I hope you know that I don't give no fucks about your past or that nigga. I fuck with you Rae, we're just talking."

I closed the space between us to take in her beauty up close and personally. I could tell me invading her space like this made her nervous slightly but when she lifted her arms and wrapped them around my body, I allowed her. It felt good to know that I made her comfortable to do that.

As crazy as it sounded, Rae felt safe to me, she felt like peace. Maybe it was her eyes and how calming they were, or how her hugs were soothing, and her smile was one of a kind. In just a short number of days she caused me to feel some things...

"You make a nigga unsure..."

"Unsure? I don't know... Is that a good thing or should I be concerned?" she asked as she gently pulled her head from my chest.

"It's hard to explain. Nothing about you is bad to me though, Rae."

"I have flaws, Brixx. I'm not perfect."

"Nobody is. And who said I wanted you to be perfect? You're real and I fuck with that," I assured her, and this time I wrapped my arms around her. Hugging her tightly.

Rae was uncertain of the power she possessed and that alone was scary to me. That was also the innocence she possessed. Her being so unaware of her power only confirmed that the nigga had done a number on her spirit.

"You make me so nervous," she admitted what I already knew as she spoke into my hoodie while her head was almost buried into my chest.

"A good nervous I hope though."

"Me too," she responded, looking up at me with an alluring innocence in her eyes.

I hesitated at first, and I guess she sensed my hesitation because she smiled before pulling my face toward hers and kissing me lightly. Once she did that, I lifted her from her seat in my truck and we traded places. I was the one sitting and she was straddling my lap while I gripped her ass tightly. The whole public display of affection wasn't my bop. I wasn't even the holding hands type of nigga for real. Rae had me doing things I swore off.

KO'RAE
I KNEW THAT I'D REGRET IT...

"No, no, no, this can't be."

Tears fell from my eyes freely as I sat on the bathroom floor at Ahja's. I hadn't been home in weeks. Once my flight landed from my small getaway with Brixx, I came right to Ahja's. Being home made me feel small sometimes, like I wasn't doing enough with myself because I was still living at home with my mom. Being at Ahja's gave me some sort of freedom. We danced with the idea of me moving in since the day she was left here alone and because I came over so often, we never acted on it.

"Rae, are you okay?" Ahja knocking at the door instantly brought me back to reality. My harsh, cold reality.

"No," I cried, and seconds later the bathroom door swung open, and she stood there with eyes full of concern. Before I could even attempt to speak, her concerned-filled eyes landed on the pregnancy test that rested on the floor beside me innocently.

"You fucked Brixx in Houston?"

Silence.

"Huh?" Her eyes fell on mine and the tears continued to flow.

"Rae!"

Tears slid from my eyes with ease, and I couldn't believe this had become my reality.

I knew in Ahja's mind she would have much rather me be pregnant by a man I was just getting to know than Greg. Hell, me too.

"Please tell me you fucked him, Rae!"

"I didn't."

Silence!

We both had tears in our eyes for very different reasons. Pregnant, a baby... it was all too much. Greg and I weren't even speaking, I wanted nothing to do with him. I had blocked him out of my life completely and here I was staring down at a positive pregnancy test.

"I don't want this, Ahja."

I cried harder. I was literally crying my eyes out as I sat on the bathroom floor in disbelief. Greg and I had been through so much, there was even a time where we were trying to get pregnant, and I didn't. Why now? Why me? I just made plans to go to dinner with Brixx in the city tomorrow. It was all I had been talking about for the past three days. I missed him, his company, and just his overall presence, and I couldn't wait to see him. That was dead now.

"What do you want?"

"Not this. I don't want this. I don't want a baby with him. How could I be so careless."

"Don't beat yourself up, Rae. I'm here for you."

"I can't have this baby." I jumped to my feet with my mind already made up. I tossed the pregnancy test into the small garbage pail we had in the bathroom and wiped my eyes.

"Rae," Ahja called after me, and I continued to walk out into the living room where I left my food and my phone.

The two of us were doing absolutely nothing, we had no plans, no intentions on leaving the house. We had just gotten home from work, we grabbed food on our way home, and we were just sitting up front doing nothing. I'm not sure exactly what it was, only something came over me forcing me into the bathroom and searching for an old pregnancy test. It was just this odd feeling that I had.

"I can't keep this baby. Why can't I just be free from him?"

I cried even harder as reality began to set in even more. I would have to deal with Greg for the rest of my life, just like he expected.

"Maybe it's wrong..." Ahja attempted to offer me some sort of hope. Only I was hopeless. The three other tests I had proved that it wasn't wrong.

"I'm just going to go... I need some air."

"Go? Go where? I'm coming with you."

"Ahja, no. I just need some air, I need some time to myself to process all this."

"Rae... I'm sorry." I could see the hurt in her eyes as she forced herself to hold back her tears. I was hurt and she was hurting for me. We had the same pain. I knew Ahja felt just as helpless and hopeless as I did right now for her own reasons. Greg was not who I wanted to start my family with. He wasn't the same man I was once madly in love with. I had been growing to hate him as the days passed. I despised him; I regretted the day we ever met.

With tears in my eyes, I walked out the apartment with a heavy heart. I was hoping that this was a bad dream. I was praying that it was just a mistake, that when I took the test again it'll be negative, but I was too afraid to face that reality.

Getting in my car, I had no destination in mind. My heart was heavy, my head was hurting, and my eyes were beginning to burn. I didn't want this to be my life, I didn't want this to be my story, I deserved better. After just weeks of getting to know Brixx, the dates, the late-night conversations, the little things he did just because he knew it'll keep a smile on my face, I knew that my time with him was worth more than the last year of my relationship with Greg.

I had three missed calls from Brixx in the last thirty minutes and I couldn't muster the courage to call him back.

I don't know how or why, but I found myself parked outside

of Greg's parents' home where he stayed. I knew I shouldn't be here or better yet, I knew I didn't want to be here. I didn't owe Greg the satisfaction of letting him know what was going on with me. I wanted nothing more to do with him, I wanted him out of my life completely.

Right on time, I thought as I watched his car pull into the driveway. Greg was so predictable, he lived his life routine based. He was very militant, and I guess that came from home. Both his parents were in the Marines. Their hard work was how he afforded this lovely house and everything else he had. I wasn't sure this man knew what it was like to go without, or to ever have to work for anything in his life. Greg was spoiled rotten even as a grown man. His mother spoiled him, so he liked for his woman to do the same. And for a while in the beginning, I thought it was cute, to be wanted and needed by him. I loved that, it made me feel good for a while, only for a while though, because soon after it became annoying and overwhelming. It was like he couldn't do anything for himself, always needing me to do everything.

"What are you doing here Rae?"

Just as he was getting out his car, I was exiting mine. We needed to talk. The thought of having an abortion danced around in my head for the last hour, yet I couldn't come to terms with it. As much as I despised the man, the child had done nothing wrong.

"We need to talk."

The sly look on his face almost made me sick to my stomach because I could already tell what he was thinking.

"You said you were done though." He smirked with pride, and I prepared myself for his main character syndrome to kick in,

"I am. Trust me, I am," I corrected him, because in no way, shape, or form did this baby mean that we were about to be one big happy family. Hell no.

"So, what are you doing here? I got company, I'm busy." He smirked and I wanted nothing more than to slap it away.

"Company? Let me guess, the same bitch you said you weren't fucking, huh?"

"Rae, you violated when you and your friends jumped me in that club."

"You violated when you were in the club with another bitch!"

"I apologized. I can admit that I fucked up. But I love you. I miss you."

"No, don't touch me." Without a second thought, I stepped away from him, refusing his embrace.

"You miss me, but you have bitches waiting for you?" I laughed and decided this conversation wasn't even worth having. I didn't want Greg, my heart no longer longed for him. He no longer did it for me, so me coming here was a waste of time. We didn't need to talk, there was nothing left to be said because he was still on the same old bullshit. I would deal with my choices in peace.

A car pulled up behind his in the driveway with ease.

"That's just my homegirl and her cousin, she's retwisting my hair," he lied through his teeth, and I could always tell when he was lying.

"You look so stupid when you lie. That's the same bitch from the other night."

I looked up and the woman I saw Greg with that night that we were out for Gia's birthday was staring back at me with a sly ass smirk. I wasn't a hater, I gave a bitch credit, she looked good. She was decent but even on my worst day, that hoe couldn't compare to me. Hands down, I was that girl.

"At least the bitch looks decent," I joked.

"You care. I know you, Rae."

"Boy, if you knew me, you would have never did me the way that you did."

"Greg, what's this?" one of the women called him from the car, and he ignored her like he was doing me a favor.

"When you were supposed to choose me, you didn't. These last few weeks though, you showed me your true colors."

Greg sent emails, text messages from text-free numbers, he was calling me blocked and everything, and each interaction he had nothing nice to say. I was every ungrateful bitch in the book.

"I was just mad."

"That's your excuse? As a grown ass man, 'I was just mad' is an excuse for treating me poorly and disrespecting me the way you did like I was the one in the wrong? I loved you. I took care of you. I made us a priority while you were out here disrespecting me every chance you got."

"So, you fucking with the nigga Brixx now is making me a priority?"

"Fuck you, Greg!"

With my back turned, I planned to walk away from him. I found myself becoming emotional. Did I come here for closure, to tell him how much he had hurt me, did I come here to tell him about the baby? I was unsure. I knew that I didn't want to be in his presence much longer though.

"Don't walk away from me, Ko'rae!" With his arm extended, Greg pulled me back to him. Again, like I said, he was so predictable. This was all a part of his routine, and we had been here many times before.

"Greg, what the fuck? Let the bitch go if she's going."

I could hear the woman and her friend, or whoever she was, going back and forth about how they couldn't believe he was over here with a bitch he claimed to hate.

"Yeah, Greg, what the fuck? Let me go." I laughed, mocking her just as I slipped from his hold.

"Bitch, you think it's funny? The same nigga you came to see about been fucking me, with your loser ass."

I had to look back to see if someone was behind me, because there was no way she was talking to me.

Loser?

"Greg, check your bitch." And that was all it took for him to curse her ass clean out. I stood there in amusement as I enjoyed the show.

"Fuck you Greg, and fuck that bitch too, ol' high saddity ass bitch! I'll slap the shit out you bitch," she taunted, and I casually walked around to my car, not bothering to entertain her. She was big mad because the nigga she had been holding down, I assume, was standing here playing in her face.

Join the club, bitch.

"You think shit's funny?"

"Get the fuck out my face and check your nigga, not me. Trust, I'm the least of your worries, love."

I couldn't keep a straight face for the life of me because there wasn't a soul on this earth who put fear in my heart. I didn't come here to argue or fight, damn sure not over Greg, because I was good.

WHAP!

She slapped me open handed and it caused blood to spew from my mouth on impact. With a closed fist, I swung, hitting her directly in her mouth over and over again. How dare she put her hands on me, weak ass bitch. I was about to beat her ass and take out all my frustrations on her. She deserved it.

"Yo, chill." Greg tried pulling us apart and neither of us stopped. She kept swinging and I kept on beating her ass. With all that mouth, you'd think she knew how to handle her own.

"Rae, chill the fuck out!" he roared, and it just caused me to beat her ass even more.

I saw her friend, cousin, whoever the hell she was, coming at me and prepared to beat both their asses. This wasn't my first fist fight. Growing up in the projects, I fought a lot.

"Get the fuck off my cousin," the girl yelled as she yanked me off her cousin. I had already prepared myself for this. I knew she was the type that couldn't take an ass whopping.

When the other girl forcefully grabbed me and pinned me against my car, I had no way to swing my arms. Using my legs, I swung them wildly, hoping to land a kick right in that hoe's mouth.

Oh shit, I'm pregnant.

"My baby," I murmured, and instantly tears welled up in my eyes while they kicked and punched me all over.

"Baby? Bitch, fuck you and that baby!" the one girl yelled, and I had almost forgot Greg was here until I heard him yell for them to stop at the mention of the word *baby*.

I had every intention that when I tired these hoes out, I was going to fuck Greg up for just standing here, and then I was going to call my brother to fuck him up some more. Greg feared Nine, he knew my brother didn't play about me and wouldn't stand for this.

"Ya doing too much, get the fuck off her. Why would y'all jump her?"

"Nah, fuck her, I hate a bitch that think she's better than everybody. Fuck her, fuck you, and fuck that baby." The one girl let go of me and I fell to the floor in excruciating pain.

"Baby? Rae, are you pregnant?" His eyes were full of concern and mine were full of regret.

"Get the fuck off of me! Get off!" I yanked my arm away with the little bit of energy I had left in me.

"You came over here starting shit. I didn't do shit to you."

"I came over here starting shit? Are you serious, nigga?"

"Is that my baby or that other nigga's baby?"

"Greg, I swear to God, if you don't get the fuck out my face, I'm going to do something to you."

"I deserve to know."

"You don't deserve shit, look at me! Fucking look at me. I hate you, I swear I do. All you ever did was hurt me. Ahja was right, you never deserved me."

"Your cousin was a fucking hater, fuck her."

"Fuck you! She held me down more than you ever did. You and them bitches better hope nothing happened to my fucking baby!" I threatened as I finally regained my strength and reached right for my phone. I called Ahja first and then my brother.

"What are you calling your brother for? I didn't put my hands on you." Fear consumed him and it should've.

"You let them hoes jump me."

Ahja's apartment was just fifteen minutes from Greg's, and she was pulling up in under ten minutes. I knew I didn't have to hold my breath waiting on her. Even if she had to run here, she was coming, no questions asked.

Seeing her pull up in a very familiar Range Rover caused my heart to beat even faster and my tears to fall even harder. I figured she'd call Gia or even Nine, but for her to pull up with Brixx was beyond me.

"What the fuck happened?" Ahja hopped out the passenger seat and ran directly to me.

"His bitch and her friend jumped me."

"And that nigga let them?"

Before I could even respond, Ahja was swinging on Greg. I was too afraid to look up and face Brixx, so I kept my eyes trained on the ground. I was in too much pain to interfere with what Ahja was doing.

"Take that ass whipping like a man my nigga, because if you touch her, I'm going to body you," Eazy roared with his gun visibly showing.

"Pussy ass nigga," Ahja spat as she wildly swung on Greg.

"Ahja stop, enough. I think I need to go to the hospital."

"Where them bitches at? I'll slap the shit out them." Eazy's voice was stern, his tone laced with venom.

When Ahja bent down to help me off the floor, I asked her if Brixx was here.

"No, he's not here. Come on, I'm going to get you to the emergency room. Do you think it's the baby? I mean, you just found out that you were pregnant literally two hours ago, Rae."

"I don't know, but I'm in so much pain. I think they broke my ribs."

"Why didn't you bring me with you if you were coming over here? I hate that they did this to you. When I find out who that bitch is, it's on sight," Ahja spat as tears continuously fell from my eyes. I was hurting all over. I couldn't believe I had just gotten into a fight with two random ass women. I still hadn't even wrapped my head around being pregnant.

"I should have just gotten in my car and drove off. I should have never come here." I cried just thinking about my actions. I was so disappointed in myself. "I played myself."

"Rae, don't do that. You didn't expect to come over here for all that."

"I should've just drove myself to the clinic. I swear, I hate that nigga. It's always something. I came here today out of spite, out of anger. Greg and I haven't had sex in three weeks. That means I'm about a month pregnant, Ahja. They were kicking me all over..."

"Don't cry Rae, it's going to be alright. Gia is meeting us at the hospital. Me and Eazy were meeting her for drinks when you called. Did you call your mom?"

"No. Just you and Nine and he didn't answer."

"I'm here Rae, I got you." Ahja used her free hand to console me. I was a wreck. "You have to call your mom. We're pulling into the hospital now, she's on shift."

"I can't." The sobbing continued. Flashbacks of me on the floor balled up while they kicked me plagued my mind.

The rest of the night was a blur. I was admitted into the hospital for my fractured ribs and refused to speak to my mother or anyone else. Nine had called me back-to-back and I just couldn't seem to find the words without crying.

I'm sorry, I didn't mean for shit to go down like that Rae. If that's my baby, we need to talk.

The text from Greg was just one of many before I blocked him for good. I blocked every number associated with him, his mom and dad too.

Ahja and Gia stood beside my bed looking into my teary eyes, possibly hoping to find the answers to the questions they were asking as I sat there in complete silence. I closed my eyes, unable to stand the stares they were giving me. My body felt like it had been through some things, it even hurt when I breathed.

"I hate to see you like this, Rae. I'm so sorry." Gia cried as she held my hand in hers. I was numb to the pain, well the emotional pain, because the physical pain was very much present.

"Did they say anything about the baby?"

I shook my head no and still hadn't accepted the fact that I was knowingly pregnant and still decided to carry on the way I did. Granted, she hit me first, but still, I should have just walked away and charged it to the game.

"Ms. Sanders." Tori, one of my mom's longtime friends and coworkers, walked into the room in a manner that was unlike herself.

"I lost the baby, didn't I?" There was so much blood, a part of me knew that there was no way the baby survived.

When I got here, the first thing the orderly noticed was the blood that covered my tan Essentials sweats.

With a somber look, Tori assured me that I was right. I had no words, just tears. I cried, I cried for me, for how careless I was being, how selfish I was. I cried for my unborn child because despite the circumstances, they didn't deserve any of this.

"I killed the baby."

I regretted going over to Greg's house and being so selfish. This wasn't supposed to be my story.

"Should I call your mom?" Tori questioned, and I cried harder. How was I going to explain this to her?

"I didn't want this baby, not like this, not with Greg, but I didn't want this, I swear." I bawled my eyes out and when my mother walked into the room, I cried even harder as she held me.

"It's okay baby, I'm here."

"I'm so sorry, Mommy. I didn't mean for this to happen. I'm so sorry."

Even with my mom and my two best friends in the room I felt so alone, I felt dark. The feeling I felt was unimaginable.

"God please cover my baby. Give her the strength." My mother prayed over me with the help of Ahja and Gia.

Two bruised ribs, a dislocated finger, and a miscarriage.

"Ma, I'm sorry."

"This isn't your fault ,baby."

Yo what up, you good?

I read the text from Brixx and instantly tears flooded my eyes again. I had so much drama connected to me. Here I was lying in a hospital bed after fighting over a nigga I was no longer with, when I had a man ready and willing to do right by me. Maybe I was stupid like Nine said. Greg was a dog. I was so through.

I had never been so comfortable and free with a man before like I was with Brixx. Once all of this was over, I prayed that he was still here. We just met but there was an undeniable attraction between the two of us and I was eager to explore where it could go. With Greg out my life for good now, there wasn't anything holding me back in pursuing what I felt for Brixx.

AHJA

HE KNOWS THAT I'M DIFFERENT...

ONE MONTH LATER

Punching in the code, I was opening the clinic for another day by myself while Rae was home for another day this week. I really felt for her, I did. She had been sad, happy, then sad again. Rae had been going through the motions after she lost the baby. I witnessed my friend have a mental breakdown. Someone who was always so full of life, always smiling and being the strong friend, was now empty. It was heartbreaking to watch.

"You good?"

"Yes," I responded to Eazy, almost forgetting that he was on the phone.

"A'ight, hit me when you go on break."

"Okay, I will. Later, have a good day."

"You too, let me know what you want for lunch and I'll order it, or I'll pull up on you."

"Okay." I smiled into the phone before hanging up.

Eazy called me at seven this morning and had been on the phone with me the entire time.

Work was about to be a drag without Rae. She was here

yesterday but this morning she said she wasn't feeling it and decided to stay home.

"Hello."

"You made it in okay?"

"Yeah, Rae. Are you okay?"

"Yes, I'm fine. I just had a headache this morning."

"That's why you didn't get up for work?"

"I have an appointment today. I thought I told you."

"Oh, what time is it?"

"It's at 12. I might stop by after."

"Oh, okay."

"Ahja, when you speak to Eazy, can you... never mind. Have a good day, I love you."

"I love you more and Rae, if you want me to ask him about Brixx, I can. Or you can just text him and see for yourself."

"I know..."

"Rae, it's been a month and you've been distant as hell. I get what you went through wasn't easy and I'm sure that he gets it too, but you have to stop beating yourself up over it."

Honestly, I believe the miscarriage triggered something way deeper than what the surface could see. Rae had battled depression before, and it had been an ongoing battle and her latest events seemed to trigger her. And Rae's answer for everything was distance and detachment. She'd shut me out and I lived with her.

"I know being distant is not the answer and it's not right. It's just how I deal with things. Brixx said he understands."

Rae would hit Brixx up and they'd talk for a few days, then she'd go ghost for a week or more. She had been repeating that same cycle for weeks. And week after week he had been there to pick up the pieces whenever she would allow him.

Rae and I spoke for an hour until my first patient came in. I needed Rae to be okay because I needed her. Rae was my person and if she wasn't good, I wasn't good. I loved Rae with all my heart, and I would never forgive Greg for what he did to her and all that he put her through. That nigga was a bitch and when he finally came out of hiding, I prayed Nine beat his ass just like I did and then some.

The day dragged as I expected it to. Rae was usually here to keep me laughing. Eazy sent me lunch from my favorite restaurant near my job and Rae never showed up. Instead, she went to pick Elias, her youngest brother, up from school early.

"See you tomorrow, Ahja." My supervisor smiled on her way out and I was right behind her.

"See you tomorrow," I sang excitedly. I was happy to be going home and I prayed Rae brought her ass to work tomorrow because today drained me. They had me doing all of my work and all of hers. I swear this place wouldn't be able to function without us.

It was a little after six and I was stuck in my job's parking lot because I was too afraid to pull off. Rae's car was making a noise that didn't sound safe to me. She did mention to me yesterday, or was it the day before, that her car was due for service and I heard her, I just figured I could wait to the weekend to take care of it.

"Hello."

"Yeah, what up? You off?"

"I am and Rae's car is making this weird noise and I'm scared to drive it."

"Where you at?"

"I'm still in the parking lot of my job."

"I'll be there in like fifteen minutes, a'ight."

"Okay."

I hung up with Eazy and turned Rae's car off. I sent her a text about it, and she found it funny because she had told me it would happen if I didn't take it into the shop soon. Less than fifteen minutes later, Eazy was pulling into the parking lot of my job blasting music. I gathered my things and hopped in the backseat of his car. Brixx was already in the front.

"Yo, what's up with Rae? She good?" If Brixx was asking me about Rae that only meant that she hadn't responded to his text or returned his phone call.

"She's good. She didn't call you today?" I asked, although I already knew the answer to that. I kind of hoped after our conversation this morning that she would have at least text him by now.

"Nah. She hasn't called me in a couple of days, I was just checking in." Brixx shrugged, and I was beginning to see that not hearing from Rae bothered him. Eazy had mentioned it to me before that Brixx was concerned about her and he wanted me to check in from time to time whenever she wasn't responding to his text or calls.

"Just let her know that I checked in for me, a'ight?"

"I will."

I wasn't one to speak for anyone. Rae's business was her own, and how she dealt with Brixx was on her.

Brixx had shown to be sincere over time. Even with Rae being distant, he was still understanding and supportive. He was a good man. I could see that about him. He may have been a street nigga, but he had a good heart, and I could tell that he cared and was concerned about Rae.

It was like the further Rae pulled away from Brixx, Eazy and I were getting closer and closer. I got to know him better, Brixx too. They were two hood niggas who got money. Eazy was an open book. I knew that he sold crack, scammed, and hustled his way into his money. Eazy and Brixx's relationship reminded me a lot of my relationship with Rae. They fought like brothers and rode for one another, no questions asked. They were both very known and familiar in almost every borough. No matter where we were, someone knew Eazy. They were hood famous, and people from all over knew them or wanted to get to know them. Brixx was known for his charismatic charm and Eazy for his ruthless ways. The two of them together though were double trouble.

"Thanks for picking me up. I think I need to take Rae's car to the shop. Should I call a tow truck? I don't know anything about cars. It started running funny."

"What's wrong with her car?"

"It needs an oil change I think, something like that. It just makes this funny noise when I start it."

"She has a Honda Accord, right?"

"Yes."

"Where is her car parked at? I'll take it to my guy Marco, and he'll check it out."

"It's parked right over there in her spot." I pointed to where Rae's car was parked in the parking lot of our job, and he looked as if he was about to get out.

"Thank you, Brixx, you are a lifesaver."

I didn't protest. I handed Brixx Rae's car keys without hesitation.

Eazy and I watched Brixx walk off toward Rae's car, hop in, and drive off. I guess the sounds that her car was making didn't worry him as much as it did me.

"I need to pick up a few things from the supermarket before I go home."

"Alright, I can't get a kiss, a hug? A nigga can't get no love, ma?"

From the backseat, I reached over and hugged Eazy around his neck while placing a kiss on his cheek then his neck, before I climbed to the front seat and forced myself onto his lap.

"Did you miss me?" I asked him in between kisses.

"You know I missed you. I always miss you." Eazy kissed me back passionately. We had just saw one another Sunday and it was only Tuesday.

We pulled back up to my apartment after being gone longer than I expected, thanks to Eazy's begging ass once we got in the supermarket. I had only planned on getting a few things that we needed for the house, and he was in here like a kid in the candy store picking up any and everything. It didn't hurt that he paid once we got to the register.

Eazy and I struggled to get the bags upstairs in one trip, but I refused to make two trips. I was tired and just wanted to take a quick nap before having to cook.

"Is she on the phone?" I asked Eazy, because I couldn't really see Rae but I could hear her laughing.

"Nah, I think she has company." Eazy smiled and I quickly dropped the bags to go and see who she was up there with. I would hate for her to be up front with another man while Eazy was here.

"Is that Brixx?" I peered from the kitchen where Eazy helped me with the groceries.

"Yeah, leave 'em alone. Where this go?" Eazy grabbed me by my arm lightly and held up the box of cereal, unsure where to place it.

"I just want to say hi."

"Bring your nosey ass over here and finish putting the food away."

Rae and Brixx were sitting on the couch in deep conversation. The sight before me brought one of the biggest smiles to my face.

"Okay, come on." I pulled Eazy toward my bedroom, leaving them be after we finished putting the groceries away. Only leaving out what he wanted me to make for dinner.

I worked a ten-hour shift today by myself and I could use a quick nap before I had to stand over a hot stove cooking.

"I usually don't allow outside clothes in my be..."

Before I could finish my sentence, Eazy was coming out of his jeans and hoodie. I watched as he neatly folded his clothes and placed them on the ottoman near the window.

"Come lay down with me. You look like you had a long day." He motioned me over with a smile as he smoothly laid in my bed with one hand behind his head in his crisp white tee and boxer briefs.

"I did, and playing in the supermarket with you didn't help."

"A nigga gotta eat." He shrugged.

I walked over to him and fell into his arms. Gently, I laid my body on top of him, leaving my legs hanging off him slightly. When Eazy wrapped his arms around me I felt safe. I was comfortable and fell fast asleep in minutes.

When I woke up, Eazy's breathing was erratic and unusual. For a minute panic began to set in, until I felt his massive hands grip my ass. That's when I noticed it, his dick was rock hard as he laid beneath me. I was lost in his eyes as I sat up lightly with my head rested on his chest as I savored the moment before kissing his juicy lips.

"You better stop that before you start something with your peoples out there."

"It's your people out there too, and I'm not even doing anything."

Slowly, I pulled myself away from him to put some space between us, only for him to use his arms to hold me in place.

Eazy and I had sex. Honestly, we had sex our second time hanging out. He kept bragging about what he'd do to me that night after we were drinking, and let's just say he was a man of his word. Eazy fucked me right to sleep that night and again in the morning. I had been so sexually frustrated and Eazy was like a breath of fresh air. We didn't argue, we didn't put a label on it, we had fun, we talked, and we enjoyed one another's company.

"Are you hungry?"

"Hell yeah, you were supposed to come in here and cook, not sleep."

"How long was I sleep anyway?"

"Like two hours."

"Wow. Come on, let me up so I can cook. I'm hungry too."

"And you better not fuck that steak up. I paid a lot of money for it."

"And if I do, you'll go and buy some more, nigga." I stood up from my bed and walked into the bathroom to pee.

When I walked out the bathroom Eazy was pulling his jeans up and on his way out my room, and I was right behind him.

"Is she smiling?" I nudged Eazy just as we were making our presence known in the living room, and Rae was full of laughter and smiles.

"Bitch, if all it took was for Brixx to bring his ass over here, I would have been invited him over."

"Sis, what up," Eazy spoke before taking his seat on the couch.

"Hey Eazy. Ahja, do you need help?"

"I do. Eazy brought enough food to feed a damn army."

We had steak, salmon, shrimp, and lobster. Eazy wanted all that with alfredo, corn, and asparagus. Rae and I cooked together all the time. It was actually something our mothers taught us how to do when we were kids. We were making Sunday dinner for our family by fifteen. If there was one thing in this world that I wouldn't mind doing for the rest of my life, it was cooking. I loved to cook, that's why when Eazy suggested it today I jumped at the chance.

"How much longer?"

"*Ezra*, if you come in here one more time..."

"*Ezra*?" Brixx and Rae shouted at the same time.

"Nah, I haven't heard someone call him that in years." Brixx laughed and I knew Eazy hated being on the receiving end of any joke.

"Not too much on him, y'all. I'm almost done. Here, taste this." Eazy was all man and still he was a big baby.

I held the spoon out after I finished stirring the alfredo sauce that I made from scratch.

"Damn, that's good. What brand is that? I need this at the crib."

"Brand? Baby, I made that."

"Oh, then I need you at the crib," he joked after placing a kiss on my neck and hugging me from behind.

"You better stop. The food is almost done. Can you set the table for me?"

"I got you."

I directed him to the cabinet with the plates and he busied himself with the small task I had given him.

"Are you okay?" I asked Rae once Eazy was out of earshot.

"I'm okay, Ahja. It's been rough for me, I'm not going to lie. I guess losing the baby was more traumatizing than I expected. Even with me wanting an abortion, I just didn't plan for it to happen like that."

"I know, Rae. It just feels so good to see you smiling."

Eazy finished setting the black oak table my mom purchased years ago while Brixx helped us bring the food to the table.

Brixx led the prayer, shocking the hell out of me. I swear I was discovering alternate sides of them daily.

"Amen."

"Damn girl, you cook for real." Eazy had only taken one bite and was already singing my praises.

Dinner was fun, we talked, laughed and just enjoyed one another's company.

"We should do this more often," I let out, just happy to see Rae being Rae. And if this was something that was helping her come out of her depression, then I was down for doing it more often.

"You coming with me, right?" Brixx turned to Rae, and it sounded like he was telling her as opposed to asking her.

"Are you asking me or telling me?" Rae laughed playfully as she looked Brixx up and down.

"I want you to come, but it's up to you."

"She's going," I answered for Rae before she had a chance to say anything slick back to Brixx.

"Let me get my things." Rae rolled her eyes before heading to the back to grab things from her room.

Even though she hadn't officially moved in, Rae had her own room here and everything.

"Yo Eazy, hit me tomorrow. Ahja, thank you for the food, word, it was amazing."

I handed both Rae and Brixx containers of food to take with them. There was more than enough left over. I even made a plate for her mom and Elias. They'd figure out how to drop that off to them on their own time.

Eazy and Brixx talked for a few before they dapped, and he and Rae were on their way.

"How'd I do?" I asked Eazy once I closed and locked the door behind them.

"You did good." He smiled, exposing his perfect teeth.

Eazy was fine. His chocolate skin glistened and was always well moisturized and maintained. He was tall, muscular, and sported a head full of deep waves. It didn't hurt that he had the dick of a god.

"Thank you." Reaching up, I cupped his face in my hands and showered him with kisses.

"You gon' make a nigga fall in love with your ass Ahja, word."

"Love? Boy, you are crazy." I playfully pushed him away and began wiping down the counters. Brixx and Rae helped clean up before they left, I just wanted to give my counters one last wipe down before heading back to my bed.

"I'm dead ass. I have feelings for you, strong ass feelings too."

"Ezra."

"Ahja... You make it seem like it's a crime for a nigga to be feeling you."

"It's not. I just don't know if you're serious or not."

"I look like I'm playing?"

"No."

My heart leaped abnormally as he spoke sternly.

"Whoever that nigga is that hurt you, that nigga is a sucker. I just want to make you happy, that's all."

"You do make me happy..."

I wasn't sure how to tell him that I wasn't looking for anything serious and how fast things seemed to be moving with us scared the hell out of me. Eazy just seemed too good to be true.

"Let me do that then. Don't fight the shit either. I can already see the wheels in your head turning. I never felt anything but lust for a female, I always wanted to hit and quit..."

"Mm, okay."

"What I'm trying to say is I don't have that desire with you. I be wanting to be up under you 24/7."

I agreed, I did want to be under him all day too. I just didn't want to rush into anything so soon. I was afraid of what Eazy made me feel and how fast I was falling for him. My ability to be so comfortable around him shielded me from all my fears. Eazy had so much confidence that it was hard to even ignore him. The way he stood oozed confidence, the way he spoke oozed boss, and the way he carried himself, I knew he was a thug ass nigga.

"You are beautiful, you know that, right?"

Eazy leaned his body against the counter across from where I was standing and just stared at me. Under his gaze I felt seen.

"Come on, let's go to bed."

"Bed? I can stay the night?"

Without turning around, I led the way back to my bedroom with Eazy hot on my heels. I may have been afraid of how he made my heart feel, but I wasn't the least bit afraid of what he did to my body. I guess we'd cross that other bridge when the time came.

BRIXX

"So, about this movie night... there will be a movie involved, right?"

Rae sat across from me in the passenger seat of my Infiniti Q60 and I could tell that she was nervous. Her body language gave her away. When my hand caressed her thigh, she didn't push me away; instead, she sat back in her seat and seemed to relax.

"What? You think a nigga trying to get you back to his crib to fuck?"

"I did not say that. I just want to know what your intentions are."

"My intentions are to make you feel comfortable around me again. What you went through was traumatic and I just wanted to help get your mind off of it for a minute."

At first I was offended that she even thought I was a simp ass nigga.

"I didn't mean to upset you."

"I'm not upset. It's all good, you have every right to have your reservations, ma. It's my job to show you that I'm not on no bull-shit. I just want you to be as comfortable as possible."

"Thank you, I appreciate that."

"I said movie night tho, right? So, what do you wanna watch?"

"I don't know... anything funny, I love comedies. I'm tired of being sad." She laughed and because I knew what she had been battling, I understood where she was coming from.

I nodded in agreeance while she grabbed her bag from the back seat once we pulled into the garage of my building.

I don't know why, but the past few weeks had me feeling some type of way toward her because I wanted to see her, and I couldn't. Rae wasn't having it. She would call like once a week out the blue and she was hardly responding to any of my text messages.

Unlocking my front door, I stepped in and disarmed my alarm as Rae walked in behind me.

"Your place is really nice."

"Thank you, let me give you a tour." I pulled her in front of me, walking closely behind her.

"You okay?" I asked as we walked through my two-bedroom apartment. In a few months I'd be in house big enough to fit my kids' kids. I was working smarter not harder.

"I'm fine," she let out, finally breathing.

"That's the kitchen, guest bedroom, bathroom, my room, my bathroom, and this is the living room." I treated this tour as if I was trying to sell her my place, and she was enjoying it. Rae found me to be a funny nigga and I never got that before. I never allowed anyone close enough to take up space in my life to even get a glimpse of my sense of humor.

"This is nice, your bedroom is the size of my apartment."

"In a few months I'll be moving out. My house should be ready soon. I'll give you a good price if you're interested." I winked and she waved me off.

"This living room is to die for. I love an open floor plan," she spoke as I stood behind her, making myself comfortable in her space. We hadn't seen one another since we went out after we flew back from Houston.

"I missed you," I admitted, kissing the back of her neck. I was holding her hostage in my embrace as we stood on the balcony, and she melted in my arms.

No matter how hard Rae wanted to fight what she was feeling, I was going to keep showing up for her and continue to give her grace. She had a lot going on and I wanted to show her that I could handle it and that she didn't have to fight her battles alone.

"I missed you too. I'm sorry about how I treated you these past few weeks. I should have communicated better. You deserved more than what I was offering at the moment."

"It's all good. I get it, you needed space."

"I did. I just needed to wrap my head around everything that transpired. Brixx, I had an amazing time in Houston, and I want you to know that before everything, I looked forward to seeing you and spending time with you. Thank you for being so patient with me."

"You don't have to thank me. I'm here for whatever. As long as you want a nigga around."

Before she spoke again, Rae turned her body to face me and the look in her eyes showed so much pain.

"I found out that I was pregnant by my ex after we came back from Houston, and it broke me. I was broken and it's so messed up because I didn't want to have a baby, not with him and not right now. But I didn't want to lose the baby like that. I blamed myself for what happened because I should have just walked away and handled my business the right way. Instead, I wanted to hurt that nigga just as much as he had hurt me. It was petty and ultimately, I paid the price. I didn't want you involved in that. I just needed some time to get myself together though. And thank you for giving me that, for being supportive even when I was being distant. You don't know how much that meant to me."

"I wanted to be there for you. You were going through a rough time, and I just wanted you to know that I was there if you ever needed me."

"Thank you for that."

A smile spread across her face effortlessly even though she tried to hide it.

"I missed your smile. I missed you." I took the moment to pull her in for a tight hug and teased her lips with mine.

"Are we good?"

"I want us to be. I know it's a lot to process with all my drama and we just started talking..."

"You don't have to keep doing that. What's done is done. If I didn't think there was still something here, I wouldn't have brought you here. Let's leave the bullshit in the past."

"Okay..."

"Yo, don't think that I'm dismissing what you went through, because I'm not. We talked about it and I don't want to keep throwing that shit in your face."

She rested her head back on my shoulder and I held her in silence.

We sat in silence for about fifteen minutes with her just glued to me. I guess we were both lost in our thoughts right now.

"Can I shower?" Rae asked once my phone started ringing.

"Of course."

She pulled herself from my body and I sat up from the uncomfortable position my back had been in for the past twenty minutes. She already looked and smelled good, but I guess she needed to freshen up to feel comfortable. Before I let her go, I leaned over and kissed the side of her head.

"The bathroom is the first door on your left," I reminded her once I stood up and headed to the hallway closet to grab her a fresh towel and washcloth. I knew she probably already had her own, but I wanted to grab her something just in case.

"Do you want anything from the store? I'm about to run out right quick. Ice cream or anything?"

"Popcorn, caramel popcorn. Do you want me to come with you?"

"Nah, I got it. Do your thing, I'll be right back. Text me what you want, and I'll pick it up."

"Okay..."

"What? Are you afraid to be here alone?" I asked as I looked at her with concern in my eyes because she seemed to be worried.

"No... I'm fine."

"I'll be right back. A'ight?"

"Okay. Be safe." She kissed me lightly on my lips before disappearing into my bedroom. Once I heard the shower running, I headed out and made sure to lock the door behind me.

When I returned after getting everything she had sent me, a good hour passed.

"I'm back," I announced just so I wouldn't scare her.

"Do you need any help with that?" She laughed as she watched me struggle a little to put all the bags on the counter.

"Nah, I got it." I watched as she made her presence known as she walked into the kitchen where I was in a pair of biker shorts and a tank top. I could see her nipples because she didn't have a bra on.

"You literally got everything I asked for. Wow." She looked through the bags like a kid in the candy store.

"I tried to."

"Thank you. You didn't have to buy all this. I was just being greedy." She shook her head as if she was shocked that I had gotten everything on the list of items she had sent me. I even went as far going to another supermarket for the butter pecan ice cream that she wanted along with the caramel drizzle.

"I want you to be comfortable."

"Thank you, Brixx." She looked me in my eyes with the sexiest smile as I removed my hoodie and hung it on the door.

"You're welcome."

"Do you want to watch a movie, or we can talk..." she asked once I finished putting the groceries away.

"Whatever you want, Rae."

I washed my hands, grabbed two bowls, the chocolate chip pecan cookies she wanted, and the ice cream she asked for and headed over to the couch.

"We can watch a movie, I guess. It has to be something that neither of us has seen before," she suggested, and I watched as she walked over to my gray sectional from Lovesac and made herself comfortable with the throw blanket.

We found a movie on Netflix that neither of us had seen and watched it from beginning to end with her lying under me the entire time.

"Thank you for this." A few minutes after the credits began playing, she pulled herself from me and I pulled her right back to me. I was comfortable and I didn't feel like getting up just yet.

"You're welcome."

A few minutes passed before she got up, and I didn't try and stop her.

"Can I ask you something, Rae?"

I watched her body language change the second the words left my mouth as I contemplated what I was about to say. This was the first time I was able to see Rae, like really see her. She was vulnerable, and this was a version of her I had never seen before. And any sucker nigga would have used that to his advantage but me, I wanted her to know that she was safe with me. And that she didn't have to second guess her every move while we were together.

"Yes?"

"This shit bussing my head."

"What?"

"You, this shit feels corny as hell... I'm not the smoothest nigga. I wasn't raised to be charming, I was raised by the streets."

"You seem to have a pretty good balance of both. What did you want to ask me though?"

"Nothing. Forget it..."

"Okay." She looked at me with the purest smile as she grabbed her bowl and headed toward the sink.

"Brixx, if there is something on your mind, you can say it. It's okay." After she finished cleaning out the bowl she walked back over to where I was on the couch, lost in my thoughts.

"You want a drink? What you drink? 1942?" I asked as I stood and walked past her to the mini bar I had across from my couch, and she just stared at me blankly.

"Here." I poured us both a shot. I downed mine instantly and poured another.

"What do you do for a living?" Rae asked. I wondered if she sensed how nervous I was. The energy in the room seemed to shift whenever she was in it.

"I do a little bit of this and that. My focus right now is building my business portfolio. I own a lounge. I partly own a spot out in Houston with my cousin and I'm working on owning some more shit. I used to promote parties back in the day, so I always wanted to have my own spot."

"Wow, congratulations!"

"Thank you. Another one?" I asked after I downed my second shot.

"Sure. Brixx, do I make you nervous?" she asked, and a laugh escaped her lips as if she already knew the answer to her question.

"Nah," I lied as I poured her another shot.

"I think it's cute. And your lounge is cute."

"Cute? That's it?"

"It's nice. I enjoyed myself. Ahja loves it, she can't seem to stay out of it."

"Yeah, I might need to hire Ahja. She be peeping shit that I don't. She thinks I should have a ladies night or some shit like that."

"Have fun with that. She will drive you crazy, but she means well. She's always been bossy since we were kids."

"Ya related?"

"By blood? No. But that's my godsister. Our moms were best friends."

"Wow, ya dead look alike too. I thought she was your peoples."

"She is." She smiled after she tossed her second shot back.

"I respect it."

"Are you an only child?"

"I am. The chosen one. You?"

"No, I have Ahja, and two brothers. Do you and Eazy have plans to expand your business?"

"Eazy ain't really tapped in yet. I'm still trying to get that nigga to invest his money and get it out a shoe box."

I shook my head, thinking about the constant battle I found myself in with Eazy.

"When he's ready, you'll know, just make sure you leave that door open for him."

"Streets don't last forever. Only thing that's guaranteed is death or jail fucking with the streets."

"Show him the way then. We all are guilty of wanting fast money, but it isn't worth the risk."

"What you know about risk?"

"I have a life. Nothing to be proud of, but I have a past."

"Oh word? Let me find out..."

"Nothing to find out, that's all behind me now. I was not cut out for it. I have a friend now who is in the feds because we wanted to be grown."

"Word?" My eyes widened at her revelation. I wasn't expecting to hear that.

"She'll be home soon, but that life wasn't for me. Ahja and I went to college, graduated, came home, and got a job."

"Ain't nothing wrong with that. I love you in your scrubs too."

I caused her to blush, and she put her head down.

With my index finger, I reached over and raised her chin.

"That nigga stupid," I blurted out after I got caught up in her gaze.

"Huh?"

"That other nigga, he gotta be the dumbest brotha alive letting you get away." I shook my head as I sat back admiring her facial features. "Best thing he did was fumble you. No disrespect."

"Why are you single? How?"

"I didn't meet *my person* yet. I think..." I was praying she was just what I needed though. Everything felt right, but only time will tell. "What kind of nigga you looking for?"

"I don't think I have a type, but I'm looking for safety. I want to feel protected, covered, and acknowledged. I want a real man, someone caring, someone honest. A boss, not just a nigga with money because money isn't everything. I want someone that isn't afraid to challenge me, push me, and still make me feel safe. I want to be able to walk around screaming, my man, my man, my man!" she went on, and I just sat there taking in every word.

Rae was full of beauty inside and out. Everything about her seemed pure and genuine.

"Oh, so you are looking for a square ass nigga, huh?"

"No..."

"Baby, I'm a thug..." I joked.

"Thugs need love too." She looked me in my eyes as she spoke.

"We do. I'm still a good nigga, I'm real as they come. I'm a boss. I'm not perfect, I'll never claim to be, but I'm loyal. Niggas lack loyalty and I pride myself on it. I won't sit here and say I'm exactly the nigga you're looking for, but I'm hoping it's something in me that makes you stick around."

"What's the longest relationship you've been in?" She changed the subject and I respected that.

"Nun too crazy. I mean, I fucked with someone heavy off and on for years, but we only did the whole relationship thing once and it lasted but a minute. Not everyone is who they say they are."

"You've only ever been in one relationship?"

"Two if you count my hustle. I'm married to the money." I smiled and she waved me off.

"How old are you again?"

"Thirty-one. You?"

"Twenty-nine."

"You gone be mine, you know that, right?"

"How are you so sure about that?"

"Some shit you just know. I'ma shower, you good?"

"I'm fine." She smiled before I disappeared into my bedroom to prepare for my shower.

I stood in the bathroom naked as the day I was born and stepped into the shower. I liked that her scent lingered in my bathroom. I adjusted the water to a temperature that I was comfortable with and allowed the water to wash over me. I grabbed my bodywash and began soaping up my rag. I made sure to clean every part of my body twice before I got out. As I cleared the mist from the mirror, I looked myself over as I brushed my teeth. With my towel wrapped around my waist, I walked into my bedroom with Rae nowhere in sight.

"Yo, Rae!"

"Why are you yelling? Are you okay?" The look of concern was evident on her beautiful face.

"Why aren't you in the bed?" I asked with a raised brow because I hoped she didn't think I was letting her sleep alone.

"I was on the phone with Gia and Ahja, and I also wasn't sure where I was supposed to sleep." She laughed because she must've known how crazy she sounded as soon as the words left her mouth.

"You sound crazy. With me."

She smiled instead of responding and walked into the room fully as she said her goodbyes to her friends.

"Okay."

"What? You don't feel comfortable?" I quizzed as I tried to read her as she stood there emotionless, just sporting a big smile.

"I wouldn't be here if I didn't feel comfortable with you, Brixx."

"So, you just wanted me to tell you that I wanted you to sleep with me tonight?" I cracked a smile and she nodded.

"Maybe." She shrugged as she watched me move around my room with ease, gathering my clothes with only a towel wrapped around my waist. I smirked as I watched her eyes linger on my print.

"Put some clothes on." She walked out and once I was dressed, I'd be calling her back in here again.

"Brixx, where'd you put the remo…" She barged back into the room without warning, leaving me fully exposed, dick hanging and everything.

"Huh?" I tried to turn around, shielding myself with my briefs in hand.

"The remote. I was trying to turn the TV off." She smirked, not bothering to look away.

I peeped the lust in her eyes and tried to ignore it.

"It'll go off," I told her as I pulled my briefs up, and her eyes never left me as she watched what I was doing.

"Alexa, turn living room TV off."

"Fancy." She walked toward the bed, never breaking eye contact, and made herself comfortable.

"Do you have to work in the morning?"

"Yes. At ten."

"A'ight."

"Are you going to lay like that all night?" she asked, and I had to laugh. I felt like a lil' nigga on his first mission with the way I was trying to respect her space.

"What you mean?" I tried to play it off like I didn't know what she was talking about but lowkey, she made me nervous.

"I want you to hold me, at least. You're acting like you're afraid to be next to me, like I'm so fragile that I'll break."

I had every intention to get into bed with her and pull her to me so I could fall asleep, but I also wanted to respect her space.

"I won't break, Brixx." Rae maneuvered her body over to me and rested her head on my chest with ease.

"In Houston, I thanked you for being the perfect gentleman, but if I'm being honest…"

"What?"

"Nothing."

"Nah, say it."

"We both want the same thing, Brixx…"

I looked at her long and hard as her body spoke to me, before standing and connecting my phone to the Bluetooth speaker. I done had plenty pussy before but for whatever reason, something felt different in this moment.

Chris Brown played in the background as I made my way back over to the bed.

Pulling Rae to the edge of the bed, I removed her shorts and then her panties before dipping my tongue in her wetness. As I got on my knees, Rae locked eyes with me, making it hard for me not to devour her pussy. I planned to suck the soul from her until she begged for me to stop.

As much as I wanted to feel inside her, I gave her pussy my full attention up until she was literally begging for me to stop as I ate her pussy from the back.

Leaving her on the bed panting and contemplating her next move, I rose from the floor and reached for a condom, pulling it securely over my dick.

"Brixx," she moaned my name so sexily as I entered her, I almost froze up in her pussy.

I pushed both of her legs back almost touching her ears as I pushed myself deep inside her.

That was it. I was already forming territorial thoughts and I had only had a whiff of her pussy.

"Mmm, put it back in..." Rae whined as I teased her, placing my dick at her opening and moving it around in a slow, circular motion.

"Say please," I demanded, and she smirked as my dick hovered over her clit.

"Brixx, put it in....please."

"I got you," I assured her before ramming my dick inside her and allowing it time to get acquainted with its new home. Rae's pussy was wet and tight and almost smothering my dick.

"Gah damn," I let out as I tried to catch a rhythm, and now it was her turn to gloat.

Quickly, I got myself together and began moving in and out

of her in nice, slow strokes. My dick tore through her as her face contorted each and every time I hit her spot.

"Oh...my...goddd...."

"Please don't stop," she begged, and it made me go harder. Rae didn't know the spell she had over me. A nigga was losing himself in her pussy right now.

There was a thin line between love making and fucking and right now, Rae was treading that line finely. We switched from making love to Rae fucking me senseless in a matter of minutes.

"What's your social?"

"What?" She looked at me, puzzled.

"I gotta add you to my accounts," I joked. Pussy that good deserved to have a price on it. She may have thought I was playing but I was dead ass serious. I was willing to pay whatever just to ensure that I was the only nigga to ever feel what I felt right now. It was a feeling that I wanted to bottle up and hold onto forever.

I popped some more shit before I fell out next to her.

"Good morning, beautiful."

I had been sitting up for an hour after my work out, waiting for Rae to wake up, and she was finally stirring in her sleep.

"Good morning." Her smile was so beautiful and vibrant.

I woke up thinking that I was going to slide in something, but Rae slept hard as hell and she snored a little.

"You know you snore, right?"

"What? I do not!" she yelled and threw a pillow at me.

"I put that on everything. It's cute though."

"It is not. I'm so embarrassed."

"Don't be. I think everything about you is cute."

"Flattery will get you far."

I watched as she pulled the covers back, and I handed her a t-shirt to put on.

"Where you think you going?"

"To work. Actually, what time is it?"

"A little after eight."

"Let me call Ahja. She's going to have to pick me up."

"Pick you up? You don't see me right here? I can take you to work, Rae."

"No, I don't want to impose. She can pick me up, trust me, she doesn't mind."

"Nah, I got you. I meant that. Are you hungry?"

"You cook?"

"I do a little something," I lied.

I watched Rae disappear into my bathroom before I walked out to the kitchen and called my mom.

"Hello son, is everything okay? It's early."

"What up Ma, everything is fine. I need your help with something though."

"Anything for my baby boy."

I explained to my mom that I needed her help to make Rae breakfast. I did a little something in the kitchen, but I wanted to do it right for Rae.

"If you would have paid attention as a child, you wouldn't be calling me to help make breakfast for whoever she is."

"What are you talking about, woman?"

"I'm assuming you're cooking for a woman. What's her name?"

"Ko'Rae." I smiled proudly as I spoke to my mom about Rae, feeling like a kid who had his first crush.

"She must be something special if she has you wanting to cook for her. I hope I get to meet this one."

"I hope so too." I was hopeful. The relationship that I was looking to build with Rae was something that I wanted to last for a very long time. I had never had this before; this feeling was foreign to me.

"Call me back when you're done. Don't kill the poor child, please."

"I got you, Ma. I love you."

"I love you more, Donnie."

My mother gave me the recipe to her pancakes, and I followed it to the T.

"Perfect timing."

Rae walked into the kitchen in her soft pink scrubs and a fresh face.

"This is safe to eat, right?"

"You think you funny?"

"A little, it smells good."

"And it tastes good too," I assured her as I picked up a piece of the pancake on her plate and fed it to her.

"Mmm, this is good," she expressed as I stood waiting in anticipation for her approval.

"This is really good, Brixx. Who taught you how to cook?"

"I would front like it's all me, but my mom helped me out."

"Well thank God for her. Is there cinnamon in this?"

"Chill, it's a secret recipe. Family only."

"Whatever." She waved me off as she sat down to eat.

"Yo, what up?" I answered the phone for Eazy.

"What up, I need you to meet me somewhere ASAP."

"What's the word, everything good?"

"Everything is everything, I just need you to meet me on the Island. Everything is cool but it's urgent, my nigga."

"A'ight. Damn, I was supposed to drop Rae off to work and sh—"

"It's fine, I can get a ride."

"Yo Eazy, I'ma hit you back when I'm on the way out there."

"A ride from who?" I asked, not even bothering to see if the call had disconnected or not.

"From Uber or Lyft."

"Oh. You don't have to do all that though, I was supposed to take you but if you don't mind, you can drive my car."

"Drive your car? How will you get to where you need to go?"

"I'll manage."

My Infiniti was in the parking garage and so was my Range. I had the hookup with my man Rico at the dealership and I swapped my cars out almost every three to four months.

"I gotta jet though. Keys are on the counter."

"Wait, are you leaving me here?"

"I'm not trying to rush you out. I trust you, you seem trust-worthy... I can trust you, right?"

"I don't know, you tell me." She smirked as she cleared her plate.

"I want to." I looked Rae over, admiring how honest her eyes seemed and how good she looked in her scrubs and Crocs. She smelled good too.

"I want you to," she responded in what seemed like honesty as I gripped her chin and cupped it in my hand.

"I mean, I brought you back to my crib. That has to mean something. Right?"

"It can... I mean, unless this isn't your apartment and you just brought me somewhere..."

"Don't even start that. This is all me."

"I'm just saying, I know all about men and how y'all get. And plus, you don't really take me for the relationship type of guy. You could have brought me back here just to fuck." She snaked her neck from side to side to add to her theatrics.

"And let you spend the night, sleep in, and make you break-fast? Fuck I look like, a trick?"

"It ain't tricking if you got it, right?'

"You must think you have jokes."

"I'm just playing."

"You really think I'd do you like that though?"

"I don't know..." I could tell now that she was regretting that she even said anything.

"If I only wanted to fuck, I would have tried to fuck in Hous-ton. If it was just about sex, I wouldn't be pressed to be in your face."

"I was joking."

"Don't play like that. I take this seriously. I want you to know that I'm serious about this, about you, about us." I had never said those words to a female before.

"Is it hot in here, or is it just me?"

"It's definitely you. It's cool if a nigga makes y—"

"Save it. Thank you for breakfast. We can leave out together, I'm ready."

We rode down to the garage together and I couldn't seem to keep my hands off her. My hands caressed her ass the whole ride down and she didn't complain once.

"Have a good day." I kissed her lips lightly, praying that she didn't pull away. Eazy may have said that it was urgent, but it wasn't life or death, so I was taking my time.

"You're going to make me late for work..."

"I'll see you later, a'ight?"

"Okay, I work late tonight but I do have your car, so I guess I'll be seeing you later."

"For sure. Drive safe. And for the record, I don't fly hoes out or bring them back to my crib."

Once she was safely secured in the car, I watched her back out the parking spot like a pro and speed out onto the street.

The fact that I brought her back to my crib and told my mother about her was blowing my mind. As I rode to meet up with Eazy, I thought about where I would take Rae out to. I wanted to take her on a date to like a steakhouse or something upscale, private, and sexy.

LATER THAT NIGHT

I spent my entire day in the Bronx and that was the last place I wanted to be. Someway, somehow though, I found myself sitting outside of Rae's job waiting for her to get off work.

"To what do I owe this surprise?" I glanced up from my phone the second I heard her sweet voice outside my car window.

"Nun. I just wanted to see you."

"I told you that you'd see me tonight."

Looking down at my watch, I allowed my sarcasm to speak for itself because it was well after eight in the evening.

"Don't be a smart ass."

"How was your day?"

"Long. I did make plans with the girls tonight though... Gia's been complaining that she misses me. I mean, I have been distant, so I promised that I'd go out with them tonight."

"Out where? I wanted to take you out somewhere."

"Somewhere like where?" I could tell that she was dancing with the idea of ditching her girls for me.

"Wait, no. I can't do that to them..."

"Oh, hell no! Gia, why is Brixx at the job?" I could hear Ahja before I could see her.

"What up, Ahja." I smiled once she was in full view.

"Don't what's up me. What are you doing here? We have plans. Bitch, I know you didn't..."

"I didn't do anything. I didn't even know that he was coming up here."

Rae stood there with the biggest smile while I went back and forth with Ahja.

"You got it. Go ahead, have a good time with your girls." I finally gave in.

"I'm sorry," she mouthed to me innocently.

"She will. I promise not to have her out too late." Ahja rolled her eyes at me before walking off toward the car.

"Do you want your car back?"

I gave her a look that spoke volumes.

"You must have a spell on this nigga," Ahja joked before tuning us out and finishing her conversation on the phone with Gia.

The last thing I wanted her to do was to have to choose between me and her girls, so I was going to fall back.

"Have fun."

"Okay. I'll call you when we're done. Okay?"

She leaned in through my window, kissing me then pulling away to leave me.

"Okay?" she asked again after kissing me for the second time.

Her mouth was closer to my ear as she held herself up with one hand on the door.

"A'ight," I agreed, even though after kissing her, all I wanted was to be with her even more.

"I'll see you later." She kissed me once more before she hopped down and followed behind Ahja, and they got in my car, leaving her car in the parking lot.

"It's eight o'clock, where the fuck they think they going?" I spoke aloud to myself before I pulled off a few minutes after.

Eazy was back in the hood so I was going to chill with him until I got that call.

"Yoo!" I made my presence known as I walked into the building lobby and spoke to the lil' niggas who occupied the space.

"What up, Brixx," they all spoke, giving me dap before I made it to the elevator.

I pressed five and headed to the only apartment on this floor that was a trap house. There was no furniture that you would think an apartment would have, aside from tables and chairs in every room. Shit, if Que could put a table and chairs in the bathroom, he would. There had to be about eight different card games going on at once.

"Brixx, what up."

I spoke to who I spoke to on my way to locate Eazy in the back playing cards. I wasn't a gambling nigga. I mean, I'd shoot dice here and there, but that's as far as it went. Eazy, on the other hand, was a heavy gambler.

I chopped it up with Eazy and everyone else at the table. I even played a few hands before I got the text I had been waiting on all night.

Wyd?

Instead of replying, I finished my hand, collected my bread, and called Rae.

"Where you at?" I asked her the second the FaceTime connected, and I was able to see her beautiful face.

"Umm, somewhere in Brooklyn. I need you to pick me up, Brixx. Ahja asked is Eazy with you? We didn't drive and..." There was so much commotion in the background that I could hardly hear her.

"See, you should've never taken your ass out there being grown." I couldn't help but laugh after watching her surroundings and making sure that she was safe.

"Can you come pick me up?" Her tone was flat, but I could tell that she was tipsy.

"Send me the address."

"Okay... Umm, and Brixx, tell Ezra to get the fuck up from that table and come get me!" Ahja was so loud I was sure Eazy and everyone back here heard her.

"I'm coming *baby*, right after this hand though."

"Okay." Ahja gave Rae back the phone while we waited for Eazy to be done.

"I'll see you in a few. Okay?" Rae looked into the phone, giving me a full view of her beautiful face with her eyes hooded over and a smile.

"Okay."

"Brixx, why are you looking at me like that?"

Rae's beauty was undeniable.

"I must like what I see, I guess."

"You guess? Don't get cute."

"When I pull up am I taking you home or are you coming back to the crib with me?"

"Just remember that I have to work in the morning."

"You didn't seem to have a problem getting to work this morning—"

"Just come get me," she pouted, straight cutting me off.

"I'm coming, mama."

"What are you doing in the projects anyway?"

"I'm chilling. Don't worry, I'm good."

"Just hurry up and come get me, I miss you. I think I'll stay..."

She didn't even have to finish her sentence. I was already

making my way out the room and into the building hallway. I didn't even bother saying goodbye, I had been ready to go the second she sent that text.

"A'ight, on bro, I'm ready." Eazy came into the hallway counting his money. I knew he came up tonight.

Before I made it to the elevator, Rae hung up without warning.

I checked my messages and found Rae's location she had sent a few minutes ago.

The ride was a good thirty minutes and when we pulled up, Rae and Ahja were standing outside among a few other people. There were other niggas out there with them, leaving Eazy hanging out the window like a maniac.

"Get your ass in the car!" Eazy hopped out the car ready to snatch Ahja out the face of the nigga she was talking to.

"Oh damn. Goodnight, y'all." Ahja said her goodbyes and grabbed Rae by the hand, meeting Eazy in the street. He was going off while Rae stood there instigating.

"Where Gia at?" I asked just so I could make sure she made it home okay.

"She took an Uber."

Rae had the goofiest grin on her face while she and Ahja said their goodbyes, like they wouldn't see one another in the morning. I dapped Eazy before he walked off to secure Ahja in his car.

"Come on, lady."

"I'm cominggg." She was super giddy on her way around the car to the passenger seat.

"I see you enjoyed your night, huh?"

"I did. Gia had us taking shots of 1942." She smiled while her head rested on the door, and she could barely put her seatbelt on or keep her eyes opened.

"1942 shots turn you to a monster," I recited Meek's line as we watched Ahja and Eazy fight all the way to the car as I rode beside them.

"You good, bro?"

"I'm good." He shook his head while Ahja continued to pop shit in the background about where he was at and why it took him so long to come get her.

We waited for them to pull off before I peeled off behind him.

"You ate?" I asked once I finished helping her secure her seatbelt.

"Yes and no. I ate the food that you sent to my job earlier but that was hours ago."

"Are you hungry?"

"Mm, yes, I want some chicken wings." With her head resting on the headrest and her eyes closed, Rae continued to tell me what she wanted and where she wanted it from, and I drove straight there.

"What?" She quizzed with a half-smile, already knowing why I was looking at her.

I ran my hand over my head in amazement as I watched Rae fuck that chicken up in my car.

"Nothing, do you." I encouraged her to eat because I knew after all that drinking, she needed something on her stomach.

"Do you want some?"

She shoved the chicken in my face, and I declined, shaking my head.

Once we got upstairs, she got undressed and was out like a light, snoring and all. I wasn't even mad at her for promising me eeverything she did and falling asleep on my ass. It was funny as hell to me, to be honest.

Instead of tripping, I undressed and laid behind her, listening to the rhythm of her breaths before falling asleep. Crazy as it may sound, Rae was going to be mine. She was going to be my home, my future wife, my future everything.

KO'RAE

Waking up wrapped in Brixx's bear hug would have brought the biggest smile to my face if I didn't feel the contents of my stomach threatening to come up against my will.

"Where are you going? It's only six," Brixx spoke with his eyes still closed as he reached out for me on my way to the bathroom. He was laid out on the bed with one hand in his boxers.

With my hand covering my mouth, I prayed that I made it to the bathroom in the hall before it was too late.

"Rae. Rae, you good?" I could hear him getting out the bed coming to check on me while I threw up everything I had ate the day before.

"That's what your ass gets for being grown. What were y'all even celebrating?"

"Nothing..." I tried to speak some more but couldn't.

Brixx disappeared for a moment and returned moments later with a cup in hand.

"Here, drink this." He squatted beside me while holding my hair back.

I took a whiff of the cup hoping to pinpoint what was inside.

"Pickle juice?" I looked at him with my face contorted in displeasure.

"Yeah, drink it."

"I don't want to drink that," I whined, and he shook his head.

"It'll make you feel better. Drink it." He encouraged me with his bedroom eyes. Maybe it was the liquor or maybe it was just me, but this man was fine. He was built like a god. Brixx did things to my body without even trying, that's how deep our attraction ran. Or at least mine for him.

"Come on. I'll take care of you."

Without warning, he scooped me up in his arms and carried me to the living room with ease.

"I feel horrible," I whined into his chest, and he hugged me, creating this sense of peace around me, and warmth. Something I never felt with another man before.

"Finish that cup and you'll feel better. Throw it back like you were throwing them shots back with your girls."

"Okayyy," I groaned once the remnants of the cup hit the back of my throat. It was horrible.

"Good girl," Brixx coached once I handed him the empty cup.

"It's supposed to make me feel better, right?" I asked, because after drinking the cup in its entirety my stomach felt worse than it did moments ago.

"Yeah." He laughed, taking up all the space in my ears with his boisterous laugh.

"Ok, I just want to feel better," I whined, regretting that I even allowed Gia and Ahja to encourage me to take all those shots last night.

"Big bad Rae all fucked up over some drinks."

"It's not funny, Brixx." I buried my head deeper into his chest just praying the concoction he made me eased my stomach.

"You gon' be alright," he assured me and sealed it with a kiss to my forehead.

Brixx held me in his arms while I napped until it was time for me to get up for work. The pickle juice helped a lot, but I still felt uneasy.

For about an hour, I laid in his arms and allowed him to console me before it was time for me to get up for work.

"Don't go, you don't feel good, right?" Brixx spoke as if it was just that easy, and he could read my mind because I really didn't want to go. I'd much rather stay here and spend the day with him in bed while he so nicely nursed me back to health.

"If only my life was that simple. I would stay here all day."

"It can be. Your life can be whatever you want it to be when you're with me," he said matter-of-factly, and it caused me to smile. His confidence in the way he spoke aroused me.

"Oh yeah?" I responded, my voice laced with sarcasm. Brixx was selling me a dream for sure and for some reason, I believed that it was one that he could deliver on. He wasn't just blowing smoke.

"I'm saying though, you don't have to go. How much do you make an hour?"

"Twenty-five," I answered while I looked through my bag for my lavender scrubs in the middle of his room. Thankfully I over-packed the night before, so I had extra clothes here.

"I got that."

"Me too," I teased as I pulled my braids into a low bun to get ready for my shower. I had a hair appointment this weekend. It was time for me to get rid of these braids.

"I'll double it." He gave me a look as if he just knew that I'd take him up on his offer now.

"I have to go to work, Brixx."

"So let me guess, you have Ahja driving all the way out here to pick you up?"

"Yes. It's not that far. She should be leaving out soon actually."

"I'm just saying, that's crazy that she's about to drive for an hour to come pick you up when the clinic is only fifteen maybe twenty minutes from her crib."

"And she is..." I laughed because it only sounded crazy when he said it aloud. Ahja would drive across the country for me, and I'd do the same for her.

"Nah, what I'm trying to say is that she doesn't have to. I can drop you off to work, Rae."

"Oh, wait, I have your car. I planned on going home last night..."

"I can drop you off to your crib so you can get it. Come on."

"So, you don't want it back?"

"I don't need it back. You don't like it? You want the Range?"

"No, I love it. It's actually the car I asked my brother to buy me, and I ended up with a Honda after we had a big argument." I rolled my eyes just thinking back to that day Nine pulled up in my dream car only to drop me off at the Honda dealership in it.

"Y'all had a big fight, and that nigga still bought you a car?"

"Yes." I shrugged my shoulders because my brother may get pissed with me but he always came through for me.

"You are spoiled."

I walked off and headed to the bathroom to go through my hygiene routine with Brixx following behind me running his mouth about wanting to meet my brother.

I showered as quick as I could, only because Brixx kept trying to shower with me and I knew had I allowed him to join me, I would have never made it to work on time or at all. I swear I had to catch myself before I slipped up and allowed him to have his way.

"Why are you playing games?" Brixx stood in the doorway half naked, rubbing his hand over his deep waves.

"I'm just trying to get ready for work. Can you watch out?" I asked politely as I tried to exit the bathroom to finish getting dressed. "Excuse me." I stood toe to toe with him, though my small frame was no match for his.

"Give me a kiss," he all but demanded before he leaned down and kissed me.

"Can I get dressed now?" I asked after falling deep into his kiss.

"Yeah, go ahead." Brixx moved to the side and allowed me space to walk into his room to finish getting ready for work.

As soon as I was getting ready to put my shoes on near the door, Brixx came out, swooping me into his arms.

"Have a good day, boss lady," he spoke into my ear as my body clung to his.

"Thank you. I'll try."

"Rae, if you don't want to go, just say the word. Arrangements can be made." Brixx pressed his manhood into my stomach, causing me to shiver at his touch.

"Stop. I'm going...I... I have to," I stammered over my words slightly as the thought of calling out and staying here with him plagued my mind.

"You were talking all that shit last night and ended up falling asleep on me." Brixx kissed my ear then my neck, almost causing me to slip out my shoes and my scrubs.

"I was drunk and tired. I'm sorry." He caused me to giggle nervously as I looked up at him, not surprised that he wasn't allowing me to live last night down as I would have hoped.

"It's all good. You ready?"

"I am. Are you going to let me go?" I asked, not because I wanted him to let me go but because I knew if I got too comfortable, I'd stay.

"I don't want to, but I will," he spoke, and the scent of mint attacked my nostrils as he spoke.

"Please and thank you."

I liked the thought of knowing that he wanted me around. Brixx was all man, he was hard on the outside, real tough and guarded, but when he was with me, he seemed to open up. Like he didn't mind letting me in, and I loved that. Having a man who was soft with me and for me was a pleasure, and I always wanted that. I always wanted someone to pay attention to me the way my father and brother did. Even if he was an animal to the world, he seemed to be at peace with me.

"Hold on, this is my brother." My eyes lit up in excitement once I saw Elias's name and picture flash across my screen.

"Rae, I miss you. When are you coming home?"

"I miss you more. I'll come see you today when I get off. Okay?"

"Mommy said you moved in with Ahja. Why didn't you tell me you were moving out?"

"It just happened."

"I have a game tonight at seven, are you coming?"

"I'll see if I me and Ahja can leave early. Okay?"

"Okay." The sadness in his voice was evident. I hadn't seen or spent time with my baby brother in a while. Between work and me staying at Ahja's, I hadn't made much time for him.

"Who's that?" I heard my mother ask, and he showed her the phone.

"Hey Mommy."

"Hey baby. Where are you? I spoke to Ahja this morning and she said you had already left."

"I'm at my friend's house."

"Your friend? What's this friend's name, Rae? Is it the same friend that you were with in Houston, and you couldn't stop talk—"

"Ma yes, and he can hear you."

"I'm sorry baby, call me later. Come on Elias, before you are late to school."

"Later Rae."

"Later Eli. I love you."

"I love you more."

Once the call ended Brixx was standing there with the biggest smile.

"So, you were talking about me to your moms?"

"Don't flatter yourself." I knew his smile had everything to do with my mom mentioning Houston.

"I'm flattered though. You told your mother about me." He smiled proudly and it kind of made me smile too.

"I did. It was before all that happened with my ex..."

"Before you went ghost on me?" He smiled as he sifted through his drawer as if he was in search of something.

"What do you have planned for the day?"

"I have some running around to do. Then I have a meeting at three with my accountant..."

I knew Brixx had money, I knew that he was paid and that this was only his home when he wanted it to be. The other night we talked, and I learned all about his business endeavors, his house in DC and condo in Houston. Brixx was a wealthy man, and it constantly crossed my mind that he'd get the impression that I was interested in him for his money and not for who he was outside of it.

"I just need to grab a few things and we can leave."

"I can just take an Uber, you know..."

"Rae, if I wanted you to take an Uber, you'd be getting in one. I promise if you'd just let me be the man that you need, things would go way easier."

He walked off to get dressed and came back in a gray sweatsuit and New Balance 990's. His print was showing.

"You are a walking thirst trap." I laughed as I grabbed my purse and overnight bag, prepared to follow him out his apartment.

"Where you going with that bag?"

"I need to take my clothes home..."

"I have a washer and dryer in here."

"Brixx..."

"Rae..."

"I'll leave it." I dropped my overnight bag and stood ready to go.

"I'ma fix you, watch."

I said nothing, I just stood there waiting for him to grab his wallet and phones.

"You think I'm playing with you?" he asked, and I ignored him.

"What are you doing?" I squealed. He caught me off guard when he lifted me off my feet and tossed me on his counter.

"Stop fighting me, Rae. Just let me in, I'm not trying to get over on you, I don't want to hurt you." He buried his head in the crook of my neck as he spoke to me.

"I'm not fighting you. Can we go? I'm going to be late."

"You are. I don't make your pussy wet?" he whispered in my ear before kissing my neck.

"What?" His question came out of left field.

"Yes or no?"

I said nothing. I was immobilized.

"Trust is earned, I get that. I'ma break down every wall and have you fall in love with me."

"Love?"

"Watch," he assured me as he kissed me sloppily, forcing me to drop my phone and drape my arms across his big shoulders.

"I want you," he whispered I my ear and kissed my neck then my forehead.

My flesh burned as he kissed, licked, and sucked all over my neck.

"I have... to go to work." The way his lips were pulling and tugging on my skin, I was sure he was going to leave a mark.

"I'm sorry. I see I'ma have to make you beg for this dick," he groaned as he continued to disregard my request to go to work.

In one swift movement I was off the counter and on my feet, feeling the bulge in his sweatpants pressing against my stomach.

"Let me just put the tip in." He playfully turned me around and bent me over.

Once his hands found my nipple, I found myself giving in as a moan escaped my pursed lips.

"Damn, your moan sexy as fuck. Tell me to stop and I'll stop, Rae." He twirled my nipple between his fingers, and I tried to find the courage to ask him to stop.

"Mmmm." A stifled moan escaped my lips louder than the last one once I felt his dick at my opening.

This can't be happening...

I was both shocked and aroused. I felt my legs giving out on me as the puddle between my legs dripped.

"I'm not coming back here if this is how our mornings are going to be," I whined, knowing that I was lying through my teeth. "I just wanted to go to work."

"I just want to make sure you start the day off right. Am I wrong for that? A nigga is just trying to take care of you. Let me do that." I heard the drawer open and close as I stood with my stomach pressed against the counter. He had me pinned in one spot.

I was too stubborn to beg so I said nothing. I just allowed him to have his way and prayed that my supervisor didn't trip on me too bad for being late.

"Damn!" left my lips without my permission once he slid inside me.

"I need you, Rae," he spoke into my ear as he entered me slowly, and that was all she wrote.

An hour later, I was in the passenger seat to his Range Rover lost in my thoughts.

"Yo, is your little brother nice? And don't just say yes because he's your brother," he asked, breaking the silence.

"You can google him. Elias Santana. I wouldn't lie to you. My brothers eat, sleep, and breathe sports."

"I'll be the judge of that."

While driving, Brixx pulled out his phone and I assumed he was googling Elias.

"Oh a'ight, little man is actually nice. I might have to pop out to one of his games."

"You should. He's a big deal."

"Look at you. You must be his number one fan." I could only imagine how my face lit up when I spoke about my brother.

"I am. Oh, and I'm going to try and make his game tonight when I get off."

"Okay." He looked at me as if I was oversharing.

"I'm just telling you because I have your car."

"I appreciate it, but do you, Rae. I'm not clocking your every move. Do what you need to do." He smiled and squeezed my thigh.

When he pulled into the parking lot to my job, Ahja was already parked in my spot, and his Infiniti was parked directly beside it.

"How'd you make that happen?"

"I had Eazy drop it off for you. Ahja has the keys."

"Thank you, but you're going to get me cursed out." I playfully rolled my eyes as I watched my supervisor walk across the parking lot.

"My fault."

"I'll call you later. Thank you for dropping me off." I leaned over for a hug and kiss.

"Have a good day," he spoke as I began walking away from his car.

"I take it you two hung out last night," Katrina, our supervisor, spoke once I met Ahja in the breakroom.

"Something like that."

Katrina had been our supervisor for the last three years and we had built a healthy work relationship. She was just a few years older than us and she was like a big sister to the both of us.

"Rae has a new boyfriend," Ahja blurted out, as if anyone asked her.

"I do not. We are just friends."

"Friends? Trina, do any of your friends take you to Houston for a first date? Let you drive their brand-new car? Cry when you want to hang out with your friends?"

"No Ahja, they don't." She screwed her face up playfully.

"Exactly. That man is more than a friend. Rae put it on him. She had to."

"You did," Katrina cosigned, and I blushed, embarrassed to even be having this conversation.

"We are friends." I was sticking to my story.

"Lies. Any man willing to go the extra mile for you is a man worth claiming. But I get it, considering all that you've been through you're hesitant, and that's expected. But don't allow your past to dictate your future. Before you know it you'll be thirty-five living alone with a bunch of regrets. I don't want that for you, so forgive who you need to forgive and move on."

I allowed Katrina's words to sit with me throughout my entire shift.

"You that bitch." Ahja had been on me all day and she refused to let up.

"Can you stop?" I asked as we began closing up.

"I'm just telling it like it is. I need what you have."

"What I have? Girl, did I not just have a miscarriage because I wanted to be outside fighting over a no-good nigga a month ago?"

"Yeah, and now, you're pushing an Infiniti and one of the wealthiest niggas in our city wants you. So yeah, you may have been down bad before but you're not anymore."

"And neither are you. You and Eazy..."

"Me and Eazy nothing. Rae, we fuck, there's no love there. That nigga is a hoe. Yes, he gives me money and plays his part when I want him to, but that's as far as that goes. Don't you dare compare me and Eazy casually fucking to what you and Brixx are building. That man has been adamant from the first day he laid eyes on you that he wanted you. I don't want what I have for you. I prayed that Brixx was the real deal because you deserve it and so far, so good."

"You prayed that for me?"

"I always pray for you, hoe. Look Rae, if anyone deserves love and to be spoiled, it's you. Let that man have his way. I know it won't be easy but try and trust him."

"But what if it's all just a façade? What if it's too good to be true? Because that's how it feels."

"Then you get back up and try again. Until that man shows you otherwise though, don't jump to conclusions. Be happy, be present, and have fun."

I received everything that Ahja was saying with an open mind and heart.

"Don't ever forget that you are that bitch! And these niggas are lucky that I'm willing to share you. Brixx included."

Brixx

"Mr. St. Michaels, the check cleared, and we are good to go."

"Good looks, Jimmy."

Jimmy, my accountant, stood before me with his hand outright, ready for me to shake it.

"I need you to move some money around for my mans. I'll be in touch."

"Whatever you need, you know I got you." He nodded and walked me to the door. I had been waiting on my cousin to send his bread over so that we could start moving forward with the club grand opening in Houston and he had finally sent it over. I wasn't the type of nigga to count the next man's pockets so when he said that he needed some time, I gave him just that. Now we were in the process of finalizing all the paperwork and should be looking to start renovations withing the next three weeks.

"Brixx, we're still good for that other thing, right?" Jimmy was a young Italian kid that I went to high school with who went off to become a big shot accountant at his family's firm in the city. But before Jimmy was this big-time accountant, he used to sell coke to all the boys in the city and I supplied him faithfully. We had this arrangement for the last eight years and it was still standing strong. Even with me getting out the game I'd never really be out because I had loyal connects like Jimmy who brought in twice the amount I made selling to the hood.

"We're good. Don't even worry about it, Eazy will take care of everything. And tell your pops I said what up."

"Will do. Good looking, Brixx."

We dapped one another and I headed out his office with my validated parking pass. Once I got into my twin turbo v8 Mustang, I peeped the missed calls and texts I had.

Just when I was about to call Rae back, she was calling me for the fifth time since I had left my phone in the car.

"Hello?"

"Yo, what up, beautiful."

"Hey, where are you?"

"I'm in the city, I just got out of a meeting with my accountant. You alright?"

"I'm fine. How did that go?"

"Everything is all good." I couldn't lie, a smile full of pride spread across my face. I felt good. I had been working hard to close on this place and it was finally done.

"Aww, well congratulations. And I'm sorry for calling so many times. I didn't know that you had another meeting today."

"You're good, mama."

"Sooo, are you on your way home or are you staying out?"

"Ohhh, I know what this is now. I's Thursday and you finally have some time for me," I joked as I looked down at my phone and scrolled through the missed texts and calls that I had on my other phone.

"Work has been hectic, and I've been tired. Ahja had me doing a double the last two days. I barely had time to do anything."

"Too tired to see me? That's crazy," I joked.

"See, look at you, you like starting with me. Let's not get on how we were supposed to go out last night, but you were too busy,"

"Something came up unexpectedly that I needed to handle."

"Mmm hmm." I couldn't see her, but I knew Rae was rolling her eyes right now. Over time I had been picking up on her habits day by day.

"I'ma make it up to you tonight. Where are you at now?"

"I'm leaving my mother's house and heading home. I had to drop my little brother off."

"Oh, so you officially moved out, huh?"

"I did. I've been staying with Ahja for years so it was only a matter of time before we made it official."

"Congrats on that, mama. Meet me at my crib though, I'm twenty minutes away."

"Okay, are we going out or are we staying in?"

"I'm taking you out. We're going on a date."

"Okay, I'll see you soon."

"Make sure you pack a bag for a few nights tho'."

"Okay."

One thing I liked about Rae was how she wanted to see me and spend time with me as much as I wanted to see and spend time with her.

As I drove and spoke to Rae, all I could think about was how fast everything turned around. A few weeks ago, I had made up my mind that she wasn't ready, nor did she want to see me or fuck with me for that matter. But since we talked, I couldn't seem to go a day without speaking to her and hearing her voice. Only thing next for us to do was make it official. I was ready to be in a serious relationship.

"Park in my spot and I'll meet you in the garage."

When she hung up, I drove the rest of the way to the crib in silence. That's how I meditated and got my thoughts together after a long meeting.

I pulled up to my apartment and found a spot around the corner for my Mustang and made my way upstairs. I made a call to my boy Ronnie to come and shape me up. I couldn't remember the last time I sat in a barbershop once Ronnie started making house calls.

"Hey, I'm on my way, I'm in the car. I had to shower and pack my bag."

"You could have showered here..."

"Hold on..."

I sat the phone down on the counter after placing it on speaker while I looked through my closet for something to wear.

"Greg, what the fuck are you doing here!"

I paused at the mention of her ex's name.

"Rae, yo Rae!" I spoke into the phone to get her attention, but she ignored me.

"Rae, I'm just trying to talk to you. I've been trying to talk to you for a month now."

I was never a jealous nigga and after knowing all I did about her ex, I wasn't the least bit worried about him, but it was something about Rae that made me want to protect her.

"Greg, get the fuck from around me. We don't have shit to talk about."

"I'm saying though, you were pregnant with my baby. You owe me..."

"Owe you... I don't owe you a damn thing. Nigga, fuck you, and leave me alone. I don't have shit to say to you."

"Come on, KoKo. You know I love you and I'm sorry for what happened. I know you don't love that nigga you're with and you don't really want to be with him Rae, I know you. I miss you and I know you miss me," he spoke.

At this point I had no choice but to stand here and listen to this nigga beg Rae for the time of day. I felt my temper rise at him mentioning me. I hated sucker ass niggas.

"Greg, you sound crazy as hell. Trust and believe, any nigga that I'm with... you know what, fuck you. Get the fuck out my face!"

"So it's true, you fucking with that nigga Brixx now?"

"I'm not fucking with you, that's all you need to be concerned with."

"When that nigga breaks your heart, don't come running back to me."

"That nigga you're speaking of is more of man than you ever were and probably will ever be. Fuck you, Greg. Me and my nigga are good!"

I could hear the tires screech before she hung up. I didn't even trip, I was going to allow her some space.

Ten minutes later she was calling back.

"Hello?"

"Yeah, you good?"

"I'm okay. Sorry."

"Nah, you don't have to apologize, Rae. You're good. That nigga still there? You need me to make a call?"

"I left. Greg is a lot of things, but he isn't stupid."

"Rae, that nigga let you get jumped..."

"Brixx, I'm okay. I'm fine, I'm in the car and on my way to you. Okay?"

"A'ight."

"I'll be there in a few."

She hung up before I could say anything, and I left her alone. I wasn't about to stress her over a situation that she had no control over. Rae wasn't my girl, but I wouldn't be the nigga that I am if I didn't protect her. It was clear that the nigga was hurt, and he was going out sad behind a female.

Text me when you're in the garage.

Rae left me on read, so I hopped in a quick shower. I had about thirty minutes, maybe more, before she got here. It was a Thursday evening and traffic was always hectic around this time.

Thirty-five minutes had passed before Rae text me letting me know that she was downstairs. I went from never bringing a female back to my crib to standing downstairs in the garage in my slides, waiting for Rae to park the car.

I was standing with my hands stuffed in the pockets of my

sweats, waiting for her to get out. She was still driving my Infiniti and acting like at any moment I was going to snatch the keys from her hand and take the car back. Nah, I wanted her driving my whip. More importantly, I wanted niggas and bitches alike to know who she was fucking with.

"You mad at me?" I asked her as she got out the car and grabbed her bag from the backseat ignoring me. "This what we doing?" I questioned her after she ignored me.

"What? Brixx, I'm not mad. I just don't want to talk about it. It's done, I really don't give a fuck what happens to Greg, I just don't want to be in the middle of it."

"A'ight boss lady, you got it." I threw my hands up playfully once I caught her stare.

"What's funny?"

"Nothing, you look cute when you're *not mad*."

"Brixx, I'm not playing."

"I hear you. Come on, mama." I grabbed her bag and followed her to the elevator. "Are we into it?" I mocked one of the TikToks she sent me a day prior.

"No. But if you keep starting with me, we will be." She rolled her eyes before a smile spread across her face with ease.

"I don't want no problems with you, beautiful. Can I get some love?" I asked and frowned down at her.

Rae looked up at me before walking onto the elevator and pressing my floor. The second the doors closed, I pulled her small frame to me and held her in my arms before kissing her hungrily. I didn't care that we were in public. I missed her.

"Brixx, stop, people could be getting on the elevator." She tried to push me away and after watching her struggle, I finally stepped back and gave her some space.

"You play too much. Someone could have gotten on while we were on here."

"We're grown, fuck them."

I didn't care who came on the elevator while we were on it, but it was clear that she cared so I was going to chill.

"On some real shit, Rae. Are you good?" I questioned her once we made it inside my apartment.

"I'm okay, Brixx. I promise," she assured me and reached up for a kiss after making my dick jump as she pulled on my beard lightly.

"I missed you," I admitted. It had been a few days since I'd seen her. Rae worked long hours and lately I've been keeping longer hours too. We've both been grinding.

I licked my lips just staring at her beauty. I was almost tempted to say fuck going out and just chill in the crib, but she deserved to be showered with love and taken out properly.

"So what time are we leaving? You don't even seem like you're getting ready," Rae asked as she allowed me to lift her onto the counter in the kitchen.

"I have my barber coming by in like fifteen minutes. We can leave after I'm done."

"Okay. Today drained me." As if it was natural for her, Rae rested her head on my chest comfortably and we stayed in that position for a while just talking and catching up on her day. It was nice having her in my arms and I looked forward to waking up to her beautiful face in the morning.

"What do you need?" I asked, curious to know what would make her day better.

"Food."

"Okay, so that's all it takes to make you feel better?"

"Pretty much. I just had a long day, first work then Greg. I just feel like the universe is fucking with me." I listened while she ran down her day to me and how the people at her job had her fucked up. And how her ex pulling up on her caught her off guard.

I didn't even have to ask if she wanted to talk about it, she was already going to tell me. I loved that she looked forward to telling me about her day and that she called me whenever she had the slightest inconvenience in her day. To see her so upset as she ran her day down to me was new. It took a lot to piss Rae off, but I guess she was at her breaking point with ol' boy and the old bitch at her job that kept on fucking with her and Ahja.

"Fuck that old bitch. She's miserable," I commented, because from the way she was explaining the situation to me, it sounded like the lady was just bored and miserable and she was just taking it out on Rae and Ahja because she was jealous.

"Hey, you never told me how much it cost you to get my car fixed. I know that I needed more than an oil change. Almost every light on my dashboard was on, Brixx."

"Didn't I tell you not to worry about it? I handled it, right? And don't let your car get like that again, that's no good."

"My car or Ahja's car? Because you basically gave my car away the other day."

She was right, I did, but only because I had her driving my car. And it cost over fifteen hundred to get Rae's car fixed with same-day service, but I wasn't looking for a dime of it back. Paying for anything was never an issue for me but always one for her.

"Yo, we're going to have to figure some shit out." I followed behind her to my room where she was making herself comfortable in my bed.

"About what?"

"About you looking to repay me every time I do something for you."

"Brixx, I don't want to just assume that you're okay with paying for everything when I'm capable of paying for it on my own."

"But you're not on your own. I got it, so that means you got it because I got you."

"Mmm, okay." From the look on her face, she had never had anyone tell her anything like this before.

"No man should be in your life and not be willing to provide and contribute where he can, when he can."

"But we're just dating, I don't wan—"

"You don't have to want for anything. I got you, that's just the type of man I am. The type of shit you deserve."

"Okay. I'm not about to fight with you." She dismissed me by pulling out her phone.

"Just put some trust in me. I got you." I leaned down to kiss her forehead before walking out the room.

Rae had been tucked away in my room on the phone with Ahja for about an hour and now she was finally showing her face once she heard me let my barber out.

"I didn't mean to upset you or come off as ungrateful. I just want to be clear that I'm not intending to take advantage of your generosity. I appreciate any and everything that you do for me, no matter how big or small it may be. It's just it's a lot to get used to. No one outside of my brother and my father took care of me financially, and even with them it was a hassle sometimes. Truthfully, I never had a man outside of my family genuinely want to do something for me without wanting something in return."

On the inside, I was smiling because she was making the effort to communicate and not just shut me out.

I could tell that Rae was spoiled but she had never been spoiled by a wealthy nigga. And no disrespect to her brother or her pops, but they did it because they felt like they had to since she was their responsibility, but it was different with me.

"That's because you haven't been with a man before." I shrugged, not giving a fuck about the shot I was taking at her ex.

"I know you had some fuck niggas in your past that hurt you, but I'm not them and this ain't that. If you're ever going to give yourself a fighting chance, you can't carry the burdens of your past here. Everything I been through, I leave that shit at the door because it's not yours to carry with me. I'm giving you the space to make your own mistakes or not, but I'm still giving you the space to do so. What kind of nigga would I be if I blamed you for some shit another bitch did to me?" I firmly spoke, hopefully shutting down any thoughts she had of placing me on the same level as her ex or any other nigga that had wronged her. "I just ask for that same space in return."

"Okay."

"I'm trying to make this shit work. I want it to work, I pray for it. But you gotta meet me halfway Rae and leave your past where it's at."

"You trying to be my nigga or something?"

"See, you playing and I'm dead ass serious. What's so wrong if I am?"

"Nothing."

"What? You not trying to be my lady? I haven't been showing you that I want us to work?"

"You have."

"So lean into that and trust a nigga. I want you to be mine and that's what's real. I'm not trying to walk around here fronting like I know I can have you, because I can't. Nothing is guaranteed. I feel as long as you know my intentions though, I may have a fighting chance with your ass. I can feel it though, so I don't trip. You're going to be mine."

With my reservations caused by my past—because Neesha's ass at one point had me on a high close to this too—I didn't want to put myself out there again, but I also didn't want to miss out what could possibly be the best thing that ever happened to me, so I was willing to give this shit a try once more.

"Here." Rae handed me my ringing phone and it was an unknown number calling me. I dismissed it.

"You're not going to answer it?" she quizzed, dismissing what I just said completely.

"Nah." I just stood there looking at her, trying to get a read on her.

Rae was stubborn but she was worth it.

"Are you coming with me to Miami?" I asked her, and she just looked at me blankly. I could tell that her last nigga was boring. I already knew he didn't have money like me, but he could have still made something happen for her. Whenever I asked her to do something with me it was like she was being asked for the first time.

My boy Ronnie came and got me right and I was feeling like a brand-new nigga. I knew I looked good too from the way Rae was staring at me. A fresh cut was essential.

"You feeling my cut?"

"I am. Come here."

"Nah, if I come over there then we're not going to make our reservations."

"We don't have to make them. We can order in and watch some TV or a movie."

"Are you sure?"

"I'm sure. I got too comfortable in here anyway. We can order takeout and stay in." I agreed and went to grab my phone off the kitchen counter before joining her back in my bedroom.

"I'm booking my flight tonight, are you coming with me?"

"Brixx..."

"Why you gotta give me a hard time, mama? We just talked about this..."

"I know, but I don't want to impose on what you already had planned."

"Rae, I wouldn't have invited you if I felt like I wouldn't have time for you. I want you there. I never in my life had to go out my way this much to show my appreciation to a woman."

"Appreciation? Flowers, cards, candy, maybe even a purse shows appreciation, Brixx. You just... you just do things that I don't expect, and I don't know how to receive it."

Flowers, a purse... So, she liked gifts? Noted.

"Just say yes and come with me to Miami, because I'm going to miss you like crazy if you don't. I want you there, Rae. You said it yourself that these past few days have been crazy for you. Allow me to be the one to change your scenery for a few days. I *just* want to show you what it's like when a nigga likes me wants you. Let me do that for you."

"What type of nigga are you?"

"A wealthy one. A handsome one. One that wants to spoil the fuck out of you. Let me do that for you."

"I'm trying..."

"You're going to have to try a little harder for me, Rae." I delivered a kiss to her lips before I scooped her up in my arms.

"When you met me what you thought? You thought I wasn't that nigga? Our first date was in another city. This is what I do, this is what I'm accustomed to and I want to share that with you. But sometimes I feel like I'm begging you."

"Our first date was in another city.... you might just be that nigga." She smirked before delivering a wet kiss to my lips.

"I am that nigga, and I'm trying to be that nigga for you."

"And Brixx, it's not that you have to beg it's just that again, I'm not used to a man saying something and actually meaning it. All of this is its new to me. I'm not trying to give you a hard time. I'm just speaking my truth so because of my past naturally I'm going to be hesitant."

"Hesitant or guarded? Because you don't have to be either one with me. I care about you, I like doing nice things for you, and I enjoy your company, I want your company, with me, in Miami. So, fuck all that other shit. I want you there,"

"Okay, you don't have to get nasty." She rolled her eyes, and I sat down with her still in my arms making sure that she sat comfortably in my lap.

"You play tough, but you are soft. You don't like when a nigga applies that pressure."

Reaching down I lifted her chin forcing her to look at me before I kissed her and she threw her hands around my neck and slipped her tongue into my mouth while I squeezed her ass. My dick instantly bricked up causing her to moan while she grinded into my lap.

"Trust is earned mama; I know that for a fact. And I plan to do everything in my power to earn yours. A'ight?" I added and she sat in my lap with a blank look on her face.

"Okay,"

"Good because fighting me is only going to make a nigga like me go even harder for you. And to be clear, I don't want to dismiss what you're feeling, I just want to understand where you're coming from." I kissed her forehead for reassurance, and she roped her arms around my waist looking up at me with the sexiest pout.

Rae loved to be babied. She was my little baby.

"Brixx as much as I don't want to bring the trauma of my past with me into *whatever* it is that we're building it just seems to keep creeping up on me..."

"It's not whatever it's a relationship, we're building toward a relationship. Don't downplay it."

"See that... that right there triggers me, it triggers something so deep rooted in me that I can't even decipher if this is real or not. It's not you Brixx, I swear, it's me."

"I want to be with you Rae. I like spending time with you Rae. Trust and believe I plan on treating you and caring for you in a way that you no longer feel that way. I want to be the man that you can rely on. The one you call when you're in need of anything. I'ma show you what it is when a wealthy nigga wants you."

"You are literally everything that I dreamed of and everything that I want and that scares me..."

"I'm everything that you *have* Rae. I'm right here, I got you." I smirked as I rubbed her back allowing her to get whatever she was feeling off her chest freely.

"You're going to make me cry and I don't want to cry in front of you."

"Let it out. I promise you these will be the only times you ever have to shed tears behind me."

"That's a big promise."

"Do you trust me?"

"I want to. I'm trying to."

I could only respect her answer. As long as she was willing to try, I was going to keep showing up for her. I didn't mind putting in the work to get her to see that I was serious about her.

"Let me make sure that you're real," She let out then began poking me all over.

"I'm real."

"The only men that I've ever been able to count on without a doubt are my dad and brother. They are the only ones who ever showed up for me with no hidden agendas."

"And me, you could add me on that list too," I assured her.

"I hope so Brixx, I really hope so."

"Let me show you. Lay down," I demanded, not in the mood to allow my words to do the work for me. It was time that I put in some real work.

MIAMI

Two nights ago, after we talked, I booked Rae's flight to Miami with me. I wanted to lighten her load a little and I figured what better way to relax than to take a quick trip out of your normal scenery. And as I expected she hadn't stopped smiling since we landed.

For two days we had been out here chilling and I allowed her to do whatever she wanted while I sat back and enjoyed the show. After business was handled all my time was devoted to Rae and what she wanted to do.

"I can't believe you never ate here." Rae looked at me crazy while we sat in Finga Licking. She had been raving about it since we landed and once the server placed her food in front of her, she had been bragging ever since.

I heard about it I just never stopped by because I was always on the move when I came out here. To be honest this was my first time in Miami and business wasn't at the forefront of my mind or even on my radar. This time around I just wanted to chill, just the two of us.

"I'm usually in and out when I come out here."

"Well, how is it?" she asked and I knew she had been waiting for my review since the food came out.

"It's a'ight."

"You are hard to please Mr. Keizer." She rolled her eyes up in the air and continued to pick at her food.

"You seem to do a pretty good job at it." I smirked, pulling her foot into my lap and enjoying the view before me.

We had been in Miami for a couple of days, and I was enjoying it. Rae was chill but she still liked to turn up. When I took her to the strip club, I was able to see another side to her and I liked it. After throwing money at ass and titties all night when we got back to the hotel, I got a private dance from the baddest female in the spot. Rae and 1942 wasn't to be fucked with. I was just happy to see her having a good time and enjoying herself.

After we ate, she wanted to walk the strip so that's what we did. With our hands intertwined Rae and I walked the strip maneuvering through the small crowd of people in silence even though there was so much noise around us.

"Let's get a drink from Kantina and go back to the room."

"A'ight. What you drinking?"

"A Henny colada."

I ordered Rae a drink then one for myself and I even ordered her some guac and chips to go because I knew she liked it.

On the way to our room Rae was quiet, too quiet for my liking so I picked her up unexpectedly the second we got in the room and held her like a baby.

"What's wrong with you?"

"Nothing. What are you doing?" Her face spread into a smile as I walked us over to the king-sized bed in our suite at the Fontainebleau. Rae fell in love with the room the first night just like she did the Lamborghini Urus I rented for our stay.

"Nothing, you seem quiet and distant."

"I do? I'm just enjoying the day, it's so hot out here and I'm full."

"This is it for you? You done for the day?"

"No. I want to go back out after I take a nap or just lay down for a little bit." She rested her head on my chest as she spoke, and I was cool with taking a nap with her. On my soul I never took naps in the middle of the day until I started messing with Rae. She'd fall asleep anywhere.

With her still in my arms I kissed her face then her lips before allowing her to lay down in peace. Once she was comfortable, I began removing her shoes before walking out onto the balcony to smoke. It was only a little after five, so I was going to let her sleep until around eight. Once I finished my blunt, I stood at the balcony door and watched her sleep from there. She was curled up in a pink blanket that she brought the day we landed from Target, Rae could do some damage in Target for sure.

As I looked down at her I admired her light snores and how radiant she looked sleeping so peacefully. I had it bad for her, no cap. My dick grew just from watching her sleep and thinking about the wild ass night that we had last night.

"Yo, what up?" I answered the phone for Eazy and stepped out on the balcony fully not wanting to wake Rae just yet.

"Yo, that old head was looking for you. I took Ahja to that lounge in Queens, you know the old nigga with the salt and pepper beard?"

"Steve."

"Yeah, him. He was talking about selling his spot and he wanted to know if you were still looking to buy and shit."

"Damn, I had been trying to get that spot for months. Of course, the nigga would be ready to sell when I'm already tied up in something."

"Word, you just put up money for that spot in Houston, right?"

"Yeah. Yo, you should take it."

"Me? Nah, my nigga, that's all you."

"Bro, how long are you going to keep your money on the streets? It'll be a good investment, my nigga, trust me. Have I ever steered you wrong?"

Eazy was not only a street nigga at heart, he really lived that life. It was all he knew.

"Never, but you know I like to stick to what I know. You think I could really pull that off?"

"Hell yeah, I got your back, nigga. Hit Jimmy up so he can go over the logistics with you and when I get back, we'll sit down and talk. This is just what you need right now, E. It's time for you to settle down and let your money work for you. We've done enough damage on the streets, don't you think?"

"I guess it's time to fall back, you might be right."

"The streets are foul as fuck bro, and I'm trying to live. Leave all that bullshit alone and build my empire the right way."

"I hear you. I'll go back down there and see what he's talking. Enjoy your trip, my nigga."

"Good looking, my nigga."

I ended the call with Eazy a few minutes later after I heard the shower water running. Everything between me and Eazy was fifty-fifty, he put in just as much work as me so it was only right that he reaped the benefits from it. There was no hierarchy among the two of us that was my brother, and I knew whatever I needed he had my back, and it was vice versa. Eazy was one of the first people to see my vision and ride out with me when the time permitted. His loyalty gained him a place in my heart for life.

I joined Rae in the shower then we headed back to the strip.

"Brixx if you don't stop." Rae swatted my hand away from her skirt as she turned the car off.

We ended up going back to the strip for tacos and drinks, and after a few drinks I was faded.

Rae changed into a skirt that barely covered her ass that I foolishly brought the day we landed after letting her pick out whatever she wanted from Miami Design District Mall.

"Brixx, can I ask you something?" Rae said, pulling me from my thoughts.

"What's good ma?"

"Are you happy with me? Is this real? Do I really make you happy?" she asked softly and I shook my head at her. I almost felt like she was afraid of my response as if I hadn't been

showing her how much I fucked with her and how happy she
had been making me. What bothered me the most was that she
was so unsure of us because of what that other nigga put her
through.

"You make me happy Rae; I've never been happier." I
admitted before reaching over to kiss the top of her head.

When I sat up to adjust myself in the seat Toosii's song played
with Latto and the words from the song began playing in my head
before I sang along to the lyrics in her ear. Rae played this song
every day and she was the reason I knew all the words. She
responded by sticking her tongue in my mouth, and I welcomed
it.

I lifted her out her seat and sat her in my lap. My dick
instantly rose to the occasion.

"Not here Brixx." She called out my name once my hand
slipped in her skirt and exposed her bare ass. My eyes hooded over
as I looked at her beautifully shaven vagina hungrily.

I adjusted my seat all the way back so that we were laying back
and she could sit on my face comfortably.

"Ooooh my gosshhh, Brixxxxx!"

She moaned when I spread her lips apart with my tongue and
dove in deep. I never tasted anything so sweet in my life. Rae
tasted as if she bathed in fresh fruit and honey.

I spoke to her pussy while I made love to it using my nose to
stimulate her clit.

"Brix, wait, please. Oh, I'm about to cum! Fuck!" She pulled
my head closer into her wetness in an attempt to drown me. It
wasn't long before her legs started shaking and her body went
limp shortly after rolling into the back seat. I had licked and
sucked her dry.

"Let's get something to eat before we go to the room." I
suggested while she gathered herself.

"You can't still be hungry." She seductively stated while biting
on her bottom lip.

"That was my appetizer, it'll only hold me over until I get the

SHA-NAY

main course." I joked as I rubbed my stomach and wiped my mouth with my free hand.

"I can't believe we just did that."

"You drive a nigga crazy mama. Next time I'm going to eat your pussy through the sunroof." I admitted as she pulled me closer to her and kissed my lips.

"Chill before I bend you over in this backseat."

"Right here? In the car? Are you crazy?" She looked around as if someone was watching us or could even see us through the 5 percent tints.

"I'm crazy as hell behind you. What, you scared? I got you, when you're with your man you never have to worry Rae."

"My man?" She quizzed with the biggest smile.

"That must be the 1942 talking." She looked at me skeptically and I had every intention to assure her that I knew exactly what I was saying.

I caressed the side of her face once I lifted myself up in my seat and climbed to the back.

"You're drunk, come on let's go upstairs..."

She tried to use that as an excuse for us to go upstairs and to dismiss this moment we were having. I was on to Rae though; I knew that when thing go too heavy, she'd more than likely deflect.

"I know what I'm saying Rae and I'm on a mission to break down every wall that you put up." I assured her causing her to blush before looking away from me. I had to use light force to get her to look at me.

We sat in the back seat looking one another in the eyes for what felt like eternity but was only a few seconds. And I wished like hell that I could read her mind and assure her that she was safe with me.

"You're not just saying this because you're drunk?"

"Rae I'm fully aware of what I'm saying. I want you to be mine. I knew that from the first day we met. I told Gia that I wanted you and I meant that." I positioned myself between her legs and started sucking on her neck. I was marking my territory, leaving visible marks on her neck and chest.

"Brixx my heart and my head are too fragile for you not to mean what you say..." she slightly backed me up so that she could look me in my eyes.

"Rae, I promise you, once you let me in you won't regret it."

I wanted her heart, her mind, and her body and in return I was willing to give her my soul.

Instead of using her words Rae used her lips to communicate what she was feeling. And the deeper our kiss became the closer I was able to pull her to me and the sooner I was able to place her in my lap.

There was something about Rae that made me want to be the best version of myself whenever she was around.

"And I know there isn't a damn thing that I can do about your past but I swear on my life and all the money I have to my name that if you ever think about giving your heart and this pussy away I'ma do something irrational to your ass,"

"Boy what? You are crazy, We've been dating for two months, barely." She laughed as if I had told a joke, but I was dead ass serious.

"I'm dead ass."

"Brixx what if we don't work out?" she asked so innocently and now it was my turn to laugh.

"Rae, one night after being with you I was willing to let you in. I never had that feeling with anyone else, you are different. We're going to work because I'm going to put in the work. Just trust me."

Allah, if this is your will, make it work. Inshallah

KO'RAE

"Y'all missed me so much but y'all are both in your phones," I stressed as I looked across the table at Gia and Ahja. "It's been a minute since we were able to sit down like this," I expressed. I missed my girls the most.

"Sorry, I'm done."

"Me too."

With me being under Brixx and Ahja and Eazy doing whatever the hell they wanted, we hardly had time to sit down unless we were at work and that wasn't enough for me. I missed my best friend.

"We did miss you though, Rae. It's like every other week Brixx has your ass out of state."

"Out the damn country. I checked that hoe's location the other night and she was in DR. Like what the fuck?"

"He wanted to go, we only stayed for two nights. It was nothing."

"Nothing? Well, excuse me, bitch."

"We had a time in DR though. Anyway, how are you, how's everything?" I asked Gia.

"My life is nowhere near exciting as yours or Ahja's but everything has been good. I've really just been focusing on myself to be honest."

"What happened with Kash?"

"Jail. I'm not with the whole back and forth with a nigga who has a fucking bedtime. He's too controlling."

"A bedtime bitch, really?"

"Yes. Kash is selfish as fuck though. It's just time for me to focus on me. I'm thinking about getting back into dancing..."

"Really? Aww, remember we used to come to your shows? Wow G, that's good, I think you should go for it."

"Yes. I've been telling her that all she needs to do is have some faith. You work in a school, I bet you can find some kids and start your own company."

"That would be so nice. I've been killing myself in overtime lately, so I hardly have time to do anything but eat, sleep, and shit."

"Everything will work itself out G, you just have to make the first step and we'll have your back."

"Thank you. But back to you for a second, so you and Brixx are in a relationship now?"

"I mean, that's what he calls it." I laughed, trying hard not to blush.

"Bitch, yes or no?"

"He says that he's mine, but you know how niggas get."

"Let me stop you right there. Brixx is not like most niggas, he's among that small percentage of niggas who actually stand on what they say."

"You know Ahja is team Brixx."

"I am. He's been everything she's needed so I'ma stick beside him," Ahja joked. Her relationship with Brixx had grown over time. Ahja was even managing his club some nights. I let the two of them be because I wanted nothing more than for them to get along, but we had been here before. Ahja and Greg were like brother and sister at one point. With Brixx I was different, but I still didn't put too much pressure on the importance of their relationship.

"That's right. I feel you. Brixx is a good nigga. When he wrote me that night about you, I should have known he would lock your ass down sooner than later."

"I'm happy for you," Ahja added, and it warmed my heart listening to them express how they felt about my relationship.

"Me too. I'm happy you're giving the relationship thing a try. I could only imagine how trying it may get."

"He works every nerve in my body sometimes, but he means well."

"Look at you sitting here blushing. That nigga applying that pressure. Get it Brixx!"

"Y'all play too much. It does feel good to have someone that I can rely on, he's always there."

"A real nigga." Ahja boasted proudly.

"Even though bitches get a nigga and forget where home is." Ahja threw a shot at me and I gave her a knowing look.

"If you miss me just say that bitch."

"I miss you." She admitted with an attitude.

I was having fun with Brixx, everything with him was new, it was fresh and fun. We did spontaneous things like taking trips on the weekend just because, driving to Atlantic City for Fat Tuesday's. We caught Knicks and Nets games at our leisure. Everything with Brixx was top tier, he didn't spare any expense when it came to spending time with me and ensuring that I was having a good time.

"This nigga is a bitch. Look." Gia quickly handed me her phone to show me what had her attention.

"Oh..." I handed the phone to Ahja without giving a reaction.

Kash was threatening Gia through Jpay. I didn't believe her when she said that she was focusing on herself, because to know G was to know that she'd say one thing and do another sometimes.

"Niggas are ungrateful. I regret the day that I ever fucked with him, I swear."

"Isn't he friends with Eazy and Brixx?" Ahja asked, and that was news to me.

"Girl, I don't even know anymore. I mean, Kash used to hang with them before he got arrested, but since he's been locked up he doesn't mention them and they don't ever ask about him."

"Yeah, I overheard Eazy mention him the other day while he was on the phone."

"I don't get between that. All three of them niggas are crazy. Nine times out of ten, Kash did some flaw shit. He's always doing some unusual shit."

"It's probably nothing. Are we still going to Elias's game?"

"Yes. The whole city has been posting about this game. I might find me a nigga in there."

"At a high school game G, really?"

"They have daddies. Plus, all the hood niggas love basketball. The last game we went to, the niggas were out.'"

"You are crazy. It's his championship game too."

"Brixx should be coming too."

"He's meeting the family?"

"I didn't even think about it like that. I guess he is."

"Yeah, you and that nigga go together real bad."

"Y'all on my case, but what's up with you and Eazy?"

"You know how I get."

"Crazy and ignorant as hell whenever you don't get your way."

"True. We're not in a relationship though. Eazy is a hoe y'all, I can't see myself taking his crazy ass serious when he's still out here doing him. I don't like sharing dick, so I think it's time for us to split."

"Me either. I feel you." I caught myself in deep thought, wondering what my situation would be like if Brixx was anything how Ahja expressed Eazy to be. I'd probably have thoughts of killing his ass to be honest.

"Ya hoes sprung."

"No, actually I'm good." Ahja rolled her eyes, and I knew she was lying.

"I don't know about her, but you don't give a bitch good dick and expect her to act the same after that."

"I know that's right, Rae. I need me a good-dick nigga with no attachments though."

"Girl, those are the worst kind. I got one for sale because clearly, he's for the streets. Ya don't know the number of bitches that play on my phone behind Eazy's crusty ass. I wish I could beat that nigga; I would be fucking him up out here. Let me even look at a nigga and he's pulling out his gun."

"Oh, ya toxic."

"That's him. I don't utter a word about the hoes he messes around with. I don't even bother myself with it because he's already doing it. Been doing it. Don't get me wrong, Eazy is a good man and he's probably going to make one of the many bitches he's fucking on happy, but that girl is just not me. I'm just here enjoying my time with him until it's the next hoes turn."

The girls and I sat and talked over drinks for another hour before we had to head out to make in time for Elias's game.

As we rode in the car, we talked about going on a girl's trip just because. I was down, I loved spending time with my girls because we always had a good time.

"We should do Jamaica. Just the three of us." I knew I had to be the one to say just the three of us because I was the one in a new relationship.

"Mmmhmm, we'll see if that nigga lets you go."

"I'll book my flight right now."

"And what's stopping him from booking one too? I don't think you're not coming, I just don't believe he's going to let you go without him."

"We are not attached at the hip. Pick the dates and I'm there." I smacked my lips because they were trying to play me.

"Nine is about to show his ass in here y'all, just prepare yourselves." Ahja warned as we headed into the gym. She wasn't lying or even exaggerating my brother would always give the refs and almost everyone in the gym a hard time.

"My mom is here so hopefully he doesn't show his ass too much."

"Yeah okay." Ahja had no faith in Nine for good reason. He was a nutcase when it came to sports.

Meek Mill played through the speakers filling the gym with his lyrics. Eli's games were always a vibe.

"How tall is he?" Gia questioned once she pointed Elias out to us.

"He's 6'6."

"He is not." She gasped as if she couldn't believe it but that was my baby, long just like our father.

"Rae what up, what's good Ahja." As soon as we walked around the gym, I spotted my brother.

"Hey Nine." Ahja and I both hugged him, I felt like I hadn't seen my brother in forever.

"Nine this is Gia, Gia I'm not sure if you remember my brother Nine."

"Hey...Nine?" Gia shyly waved at Nine causing me and Ahja to both look at her oddly.

"Gia... what's good." Nine reached around us with his arms opened for a hug and she accepted.

"Where's mommy?" I broke the awkward silence among us in search for my mother.

"She should be on her way inside."

We stood and spoke with Nine for a little while longer before I went to say hi to Elias with Ahja and Gia in tow.

"I may or may not have fucked y'all brother..." Gia blurted out as we were looking for a seat leaving Nine standing courtside with his friends.

"Whose brother?" I asked in shock.

"Yours."

"What do you mean may or may not have fucked him? It's either you did or you didn't..." Ahja looked at her skeptically and I was also unsure what she meant by her statement.

"It was about a year ago, I was out one night for drinks and one thing led to another, I guess. It's a blur, but I'm almost sure we fucked."

"Eww, hoe ass."

"Don't *ew* me hoe. Your brother is fine as hell. I knew his ass looked familiar. I was drunk, it was a fun night."

"My brother though, G?" I couldn't do anything but laugh as Gia ran down that night to us.

"I didn't know he was your brother when I fucked him. Where the hell have you been hiding him?"

"Nine lives his own life girl, and last year was when he was fresh home from prison. You must have a thing for jailbirds." I joked and Gia gave me the finger.

"I might. I see why I fucked his ass on the first night. I'm sober and I'll fuck him right now."

"G!"

"I'm just being honest. We're girls right, I should be able to tell you hoes any and everything with no judgment attached. I swear I didn't know that was your brother, I mean I always knew you had an older brother I just didn't know it was him..."

"Well now you know. And stop looking at him like that."

"Girl we are grown, I might have to spin the block on that one."

"Whatever you do just keep me out of it." I was washing my hands of this conversation, right here and now. Gia and Nine were two grown and consenting adults so what they did was on them.

"Oh, look there goes your boo thang." Gia pointed out causing me to look up to see Brixx walking through the gym doors looking fine as ever.

My face lit up at the sight of him. When he and I spoke earlier he mentioned that he'd stop by, and I didn't think that he would. Brixx dapped a couple of people up on his way over to where we were sitting front row thanks to Elias's coach making space for us.

Coach Dee always looked out. He knew Elias liked for us to be front and center at every game.

"They cool?" Ahja asked as we watched Brixx and Nine dap in a brotherly like way.

"I always wondered if Brixx and Nine knew one another, I just never asked."

"Well, there's your answer."

"It's a family reunion in here tonight." Gia joked as she lustfully watched my brother across the court.

Brixx was so caught up in whatever he and Nine were talking about that he never made it over to where we were sitting. He tossed us a head nod and I would catch him staring my way periodically.

We were almost into half time; my mother was here sitting beside me helping me cheer Elias on along with Gia and Ahja.

"Is that your *friend*?" My mother nodded in Brixx's direction where he and Nine stood coaching from the sidelines.

"Yes," I answered truthfully because she had been asking about Brixx for about a month now."

"He's cute. I hope he's treating you right."

"He is."

"That's all I care about. Your brother was just on the phone with me yesterday asking if I knew who you were dating."

"Why is he all in my business?"

"When hasn't he been in your business? It seems the two of them get along well."

"I guess." I shrugged because I was still unsure of the extent of their relationship.

The game seemed like it was never going to end, and it was so intense. Elias's team was down thirty then up fifteen, then down by three. I had witnessed my little brother play regularly but tonight Elias really showed out. With him hitting the game-winning shot, the entire gym went crazy after that.

"Come on, it's about to be a damn riot in here," I let out and led the way outside before any commotion erupted. Naturally, the opposing team was in an uproar because they lost, and we were in Canarsie, and they didn't know how to act over her. Once I saw Nine and his friends surrounding Elias, I knew that he was in good hands, so we headed out and waited for them outside.

"There goes my baby boy right there. Congratulations!" My mother hugged and congratulated Elias as soon as she spotted him coming out the building with Nine and Brixx.

"Yo, you don't see me standing here?" Brixx was standing near Nine with his hands stuffed in his sweater pockets. He had on a pair of denim jeans, a blue NY Yankee fitted cap, and a gray Dior hoodie with his chains hanging outside his hoodie dancing under the nights sky. On his feet he wore Christian Dior B22 sneakers.

"Oh, so you see me now?" I joked and playfully and pulled away from him after he pulled me to him.

"I was chopping it up with my mans and got caught up with the game. Your little brother is a'ight," he said with a playful tone and a smile.

"Just a'ight? I told you put the bread up," Elias jumped in. I'm guessing they were getting acquainted while we were outside waiting on them to come out.

"So Ko'Rae, are you going to introduce me to your friend or do I have to introduce myself?" My mother waltzed her way over to us, commanding the attention of anyone in her sights.

"Rae, I thought Ahja was your only sister?" Brixx flirted, and I always told him flattery would get him far. And the second the words left his mouth, my mother was smiling from ear to ear.

"She is. Brixx, this is my mother, Kimora. Mom, this is Brixx."

"Adonis. It's nice to meet you, ma'am." Brixx held his hand out, introducing himself to my mother.

"Don't be flirting with my mother, nigga," Nine chimed in, causing my mother to wave him off as Brixx kissed the back of her hand.

Brixx had my mother blushing like a high school girl with a crush.

"Oh Nine, stop, Mama gotta have a life too." My mom mocked the notable line from the movie *Baby Boy*.

While my mom, Brixx, and Nine were caught up in their conversation, I took the time to join Ahja and Gia where they were congratulating Elias on his big win.

"Thirty points!" Ahja congratulated Eli, and I could tell by the smile on his face that he was loving all the attention he was receiving.

"Yo, let's go get something to eat," Nine suggested. It wasn't unusual for us to go out to eat after one of Elias's games, we did it often. it was just the way Nine and Gia were constantly sneaking glances at one another that caught me off guard.

"You sliding?" Nine asked Brixx, and he agreed while letting us know that Eazy was going to meet us there.

"He does not have to come," Ahja huffed as we were making our way to the car.

There was something about her demeanor that I didn't pick up on earlier when his name was mentioned that alerted me.

"What happened that fast?"

"Nothing. Where are we going to eat at? They better have security."

"Please don't start a fight with Nine here, you know how he gets."

Nine had always been protective of us since we were kids.

"He better not say shit to me then."

I dropped it and decided to focus in on Gia. I needed a little more context on my brother.

"So, who's going first?" I asked once we were in the car. I was still driving Brixx's Infinity like it was mine.

"I don't have anything to say." Ahja didn't even bother pulling her eyes from her phone. She was typing away.

"I'll go, because it's exactly what I said it was. A one-night stand. Some of the best sex I ever had too. I mean, I would see him around and we'd speak casually but it was never anything more than that. I didn't mean no disre—"

"Bitch, we are all grown. If you want to sleep with my brother that's on you." I laughed only because Gia was acting like I was going to flip because she slept with my brother. I just wanted the tea. Nine usually went for low budget females who he could walk all over. Gia wasn't his type or at least I didn't think she was because she wasn't someone, he could tell what to do and where not to go.

"Oh, I thought you were coming for me." She rolled her eyes playfully and we talked more about her crushing on my brother since seeing him in the gym.

"Ahja, you've been really quiet. What happened that fast?"

"Nothing..."

"I know when you're lying but if you don't want to talk about it, you don't have to. I'm here for you whenever you're ready," I assured her as I locked eyes with her through the rearview mirror.

"Eazy got somebody pregnant, and I don't know how I feel about that." Ahja dropped something so heavy that I almost wanted to pull over.

"Wait, so he's been fucking bitches raw while fucking with you?" Gia's tone held all the distaste she had for the situation.

"I'm not defending him or anything, but allegedly it was before me, so he says, and he's not sure if it's his kid or not. He said that the girl just randomly wrote him a week ago." Ahja shrugged, and I could tell that the news was bothering her more than she was willing to let on.

"I'm not delusional y'all, but I also sat there and watched that man cry in front of me, so I don't know... I don't even know if I should be mad or just charge it to the game. I mean, I was the one screaming that this was just sex from the very first time we had sex. I can't really be mad at him, right?"

"You can if it was more than just sex."

"We were supposed to just be having fun. I won't lie like I don't care about him, because I do. And I knew from the jump that he was doing him. Hell, I was the one who encouraged it. I was doing me too even though he threw a damn fit whenever he heard something that I was doing. But damn, a baby... What the fuck."

"I feel you. A baby isn't just one of those things that you can just look past. A baby is serious, it's permanent, and if she just hit him up out the blue, that means she's not even sure if it's his," Gia spoke her peace, and I kept my eyes on the road as I processed everything.

"Right. I don't know what to think or how or feel, to be honest. He just dropped money off to me this morning and tried to talk about it, but I'm not ready to talk about it."

"Do you want me to tell Brixx that he shouldn't come?" I asked, instantly looking to protect her because if she didn't want to be around him then she shouldn't have to be.

"No. You don't have to do that, Rae. Eazy and I are in a weird space right now but it's cool, he can come. I'm tripping. I don't want to make a scene. I know it's fucking him up that he hurt me. And can I even really be hurt? He's not my nigga."

"Ahja, you can feel whatever you want to feel. Those are your feelings and you're entitled to feel how you feel," Gia assured her, and I agreed.

The car was silent for a few minutes before Gia dropped a bomb on us.

"Wait, what did you just say, Kash is what?" I asked in surprise after processing what she had just dropped on us.

"Kash is married." She sighed and we locked eyes through the rearview mirror.

"Wait, we've been together all day, casually talking, chilling, and the both of you have bene holding on to something so big. Why?"

I couldn't seem to wrap my head around it. There was no way I would have been able to hold information in that long.

"Because you just seemed so happy. We haven't met up in a minute and truthfully, I wanted to forget it and act like the shit was a lie anyway. But I'm done protecting niggas who don't protect me. I got a call and I did my own research, he's married."

"Damn G. I'm sorry."

"Don't be. Fuck Kash. I mean, I was hurt. I won't sit here and act like I wasn't butt hurt when I found out, but it's perfect timing. Summer is here and I'm outside, bitch."

"Mood." Ahja dapped Gia and I continued to drive.

"Back outside, girls!" They continued to hype one another up before Gia dropped another bomb.

"Oh, and ya wouldn't guess who that nigga is married to."

"Who?" I asked, wanting to get the tea before we pulled up to our destination.

"Brixx's ex, Neesha."

"Who? Bitch, you're lying. Weren't they friends?"

"Yes. I met Brixx through Kash. Niggas be trifling."

"Bitches too, because she knew better."

"Wow," was all I had to say.

"You think he knows?" I countered.

"If I know, more than likely he knows. I guess the bitch must've posted something on social media. Everybody knows. That nigga doesn't care though. Neesha snaked Brixx long before she started messing with his homeboy."

"It's crazy because Kash had started moving weird a few months ago, but whole time I'm thinking it's because he was jealous that I was outside having fun and he heard something about what I was doing. Low and behold, this nigga was snaking his own fucking friend. That's foul."

"How close were Brixx and Kash?" Ahja asked the question that I was just thinking.

"Close. You hardly saw one without the other at a time. When Kash first got locked up it was Brixx who was dropping money off to me and his mom."

"Damn, that's foul."

Gia ran down everything to us and I sat there in shock hearing how the story unfolded. I didn't even know where we were going,

I was just driving at this point waiting for Nine to send me the address.

"Damn Gi, that's messed up. Are you okay? I know how you felt about Kash."

"Rae I'm hurt but at the same time I'm happy as fuck that I found out when I did. Kash would have had me out here looking stupid because knowing him his ass would have come home to me still and acted as if he wasn't married to that bitch. Everything happens for a reason because I was so close to finally giving in and just settling down because his date was getting closer and closer. Trust and believe I know that I wasn't the only bitch he was messing with..."

Peaches

The text from Nine popped up on my screen while I listened to Gia and Ahja talk.

When we pulled up, we parked on the side block and the three of us headed out together. As we walked up the block we could see my mom, Elias, Nine and Eazy standing out front. We agreed that after this the three of us were going to head to Ahja's and just talk. I know they needed it.

"What up y'all." Eazy hugged us. The tension out here was thick between the two of them, then you had my brother eyeing Gia hungrily.

While we stood outside waiting for them to make space for a table of eight, I wondered if Brixx knew about Kash and Neesha. I mean the streets talked, there was a chance that he knew and just wasn't saying anything about it.

We sat down and of course Gia and Ahja sat with me while Eazy and Nine had an intense stare down with the both of them. It was like the four of them were having a conversation with their body language and it was intense. Meanwhile Brixx, my mom and Elias were wrapped up in their own conversation at the other end of the table.

For the most part we enjoyed one another's company. I was glad that everyone was able to put the drama to the side to celebrate Elias.

On the way out Nine pulled me to the side to press me about Brixx.

"Why you ain't tell me you were fucking with Brixx?"

"I didn't think you wanted to know who I was talking to. You told me to stop telling you..."

"I told you to stop fucking with that weak ass nigga."

"I did."

"Brixx that's my nigga though. I'ma stay out ya shit though, you grown and I gotta respect that."

"I'll always need my brother though Nine."

"And I'll always be here. What's good with your friend? Where you been hiding her at?"

"Funny she said the same thing about you. Gia's been my friend since high school though, you weren't home at that time though."

"It's really a small ass world."

"Sure is."

"So Eazy fuck with Ahja? They into it?"

"That's her story to tell."

"Who the fuck told y'all to grow up? I'm not trying to be beefing with my niggas behind ya."

"Let's pray that it never gets to that."

"Tell ya friend to holla at me though."

"You tell her, I'm not trying to be beefing with my friend behind you," I mocked him, and he waved me off.

"It's not even like that. I been looking for her ass for a year, Rae."

"You are lying."

"Word to mommy. I was drunk as fuck that night, but I remember that ass anywhere."

"TMI." I rolled my eyes playfully and continued to talk to my brother while my mom and Elias said their goodbyes.

As I stood beside Nine, I watched how Brixx interacted with my mother and brother and it warmed my heart. My mother couldn't stand Greg, she never cared to be around him even in the beginning yet here she was inviting Brixx over for dinner.

"A'ight ya niggas be safe, I'm out." Nine walked over to dap Eazy and Brixx before hugging Ahja and saying something to Gia that made her smile.

"Yo G, I need to holla at you about something." In unison, Gia and Ahja locked eyes with me and I knew we were all thinking the same thing.

So, he did know.

While Gia walked off to talk with Brixx, I was left here in the middle of whatever Eazy and Ahja had going on.

"Ayo Rae, talk to your friend before I fuck her up. I'ma leave before I do or say some shit I'll regret." Eazy wasn't his usual bubbly self and it showed in the way he carried himself. There were no jokes being cracked today, no smiles. He wasn't going for any of it and the tone of his voice right now let me know that he wasn't happy as he walked off.

"Whatever nigga. Bye, better pray your dick don't fall off," Ahja shot back as she watched him walk down the block to his car. He didn't even bother talking to Brixx and Gia, he just kept on walking without saying a word.

"He is real life crazy. He wants to beef with me because he fucked up. Niggas kill me." Ahja rolled her eyes, and I offered her a listening ear.

Today had turned out to be something. It wasn't our ordinary day when we all decided to hang out, we went from having a good time to *this*, whatever this was. First Gia dropped the bomb that she slept with my brother, then Ahja told us about the baby and then Gia told us about Kash and Neesha.

"Are you okay?" I asked her, because I knew she was going to act like she didn't care.

"I'm fine. We need to stop at the smoke shop. I need coal for my hookah."

"Okay."

I stayed by Ahja's side while Brixx and Gia spoke up the block.

"Are you okay?" I asked Gia once she was back

"I'm fine he didn't tell me anything that I didn't already know. It is what it is." Gia shrugged and began heading back to the car with Ahja.

"So, you were about to leave without saying anything to me?" He questioned looking down at me causing my body to shiver.

"No, I was waiting for you to finish talking to G."

Brixx was wearing a pair of WHO DECIDES WAR Jeans, a KAPITAL T-shirt, and the Travis Scott Fragments with a big Cuban link chain around his neck. His bedroom eyes lured me in every time, causing me to want to melt in his arms.

My man, my man, my man.

"I know her big mouth ass told you," he let out, wrapping me in his arms.

"Told me what?" I asked with a smile, and he shook his head.

"About that flaw shit her nigga supposed to be on. That's her story to tell Rae, don't look at me like that."

"I just find it funny how you want to know every little thing Greg says or does but you don't think you should tell me that your ex is married to your friend... You know what, forget it. I'll see you later."

Ahja was calling for me to come. She was already aggravated and agitated after her conversation with Eazy.

"That nigga is not my friend."

"Okay. Later Brixx."

"Later? So you leaving? Where you going?"

"Out," I shot back, knowing that I was only going home for drinks and hookah with Gia and Ahja.

"Word? That's how you moving?" He smirked as I stepped back.

"Yup."

"Make sure you pick up your fucking phone or I'm pulling up to wherever you at. Know that."

"Whatever. Be safe and go check on your friend. I think him and Ahja are into it."

"Again. Not my business, Rae."

I gave him a look that could kill and he just stood there smiling at me.

"That's your friend."

"That nigga is a grown man. He's good. Ahja just has him in his feelings and that's good for his ass. I tried to tell him to tighten up a long time ago." He shrugged as if he was so unbothered by it all.

"Well, just make sure that you keep your dick in your pants and don't go marrying any of my best friends."

"Fuck outta here. Call me when you're ready to come home."

"I will be home... already."

"Yeah, okay, be safe and tell Eazy that I said to just be patient. Ahja is my business."

"She got that nigga losing his mind. I'll go check on him if it makes you feel better."

"It will.." He dismissed my comment by sticking his tongue in my mouth before walking me across the street to the girls.

"I didn't mean to cause you any drama Rae." Gia looked me in my eyes through the rearview and I genuinely felt for her. The sadness was evident in her eyes. Her and Kash may have been on the rocks, but she clearly still had feelings.

"Gi, I am fine. We're fine."

"Gi don't pay her ass any mind. She'll be over there tonight. Her and that man are forever good. Brixx don't play about Rae like these niggas keep playing with us."

"I can't believe that Kash played me y'all. That nigga hurt me, why would he do me like that?" Gia cried and I knew she had been holding back her tears trying to be strong when it was eating her up inside.

All the years that I've known Gia, I had never seen her shed a tear until today.

"I loved him. I still do..."

"Gi do you really love him, or did you love the thought of him? Let's be for real what did Kash do for you? That nigga would call you and stress you the fuck out. Yes, he sent money and kept your bills paid but the disrespect speaks volumes to the love he so called had for you. No matter what his reasoning is he violated. Fuck love!"

I couldn't tell if Ahja was just projecting what she was feeling or if she was just keeping it real with her girl. There was a thin line because she was also in her feeling with Eazy allegedly having a baby on the way.

"Ahja might be right Gi, do you really love him? Did he ever really love you? Brixx told me something before, he said that loyalty was more important than love and I didn't understand him at first but right now I'm with Ahja because if he really truly cared for you his loyalty would have always been to you."

"It just hurts so bad. Why does it have to hurt so bad."

"Gi leave it alone while you can. If he could do that to you after all that you've done for him just imagine what he's capable of. And yes I know my track record isn't the best but just like you and Ahja couldn't stand to see me hurt behind Greg I can't stand to see you hurt behind Kash."

"Why can't I just meet a nigga who's real, someone who's honest and doesn't play games. I deserve that, I know I may flash out sometimes but damn does a bitch not deserve to be happy and loved correctly..."

"What really sucks is that when a good nigga finally comes along, they are the ones who suffer from our past the most. Eazy has been everything a bitch dreamed of, and I ran that nigga right into the arms of the next bitch who could possibly be having his baby just because I was afraid to love him the way he claimed to want to love me. That man loves me y'all and the more that I try to fight it the harder he loves on me. It's niggas like Eazy and Brixx that don't come around too often to love on a bitch that has been broken and are willing to pick up the pieces to a mess that they didn't make. And men like Nine who have to sit and watch us go through it. When Nine found out that I was messing around with Eazy he sent me the thumbs up emoji and told me it was about time that I stopped fucking with weak niggas. And all it did was make me run from Eazy even more because I felt he was too good to be true..."

Hearing Ahja express herself caused my mind to drift to Brixx and how grateful that I was to have him in my life. I didn't want to end up in a situation similar to the one Ahja was in simply because I was too afraid to love and care for him back. Brixx had been extremely patient with me and the last thing I wanted was to lose him over something stupid, especially not to another bitch.

"Rae I've been telling you that Brixx is the one. I pray he's the nigga you marry and have to go through life with because you deserve that, you deserve him. Niggas like him are hard to come by, cherish that man and don't give a fuck about who thinks what. Not Greg, not the streets and especially not his trifling ass ex. I'm about to lose a nigga that I really care for because I was afraid, and I'd rather play games. don't be like me be better."

"Ahja, can I spend the night here? I know this hoe is about to run off on you anyway."

"Yes, girl you are always welcome to stay. Rae doesn't sleep here anyway."

"Not too much on me. And I'm staying for a while."

"Mmhmm. She'll be leaving in an hour tops."

ME: *Where are you?*

HIM: *The Hood, why what's up?*

ME: *Go home, I'll meet you there. I'm leaving in a few.*

HIM: *A'ight.*

NINE

"Hey, babe, do you want anything to eat?"

"Nah, I'm good. Good looking though."

I barely looked up from my phone to give Tahira a response. I was too busy going back and forth with Gia about letting me take her out. With no help from my little sister, I had to go digging through my DMs to find her IG, and after a two weeks of being subjected to only hitting her through the DM, I finally got her number.

"Nine!"

"Yeah?" I quickly sent Gia another message asking her to let me take her out once she got off work, before I put my phone down and gave Tahira my undivided attention.

"Yeah? Why are you acting like I'm bothering you but you were the one who asked to come over here? It wasn't the other way around." She rolled her eyes as I stood up from my seat.

"Ayo, chill out with all that attitude. I'm here, right?"

"Barely."

"What are you making?" I asked, dismissing her opportunity to argue.

"I'm not making anything because you just said that you

weren't hungry." Tahira was full of attitude on the regular so today wasn't any different from any other day with her.

"Make some chicken and waffles."

"Are you serious?"

"Come on, Tah baby, feed a nigga. I'm hungry. Don't I always feed you when you ask? I never leave you hungry, ma."

"Nine, you feed me with dick and more problems. And please don't stand here and act like I'm tripping for no reason, because you've been on your phone since you got here." She waved me off before heading out her bedroom, and naturally I followed behind her, eager to see if she would fold or not. Every day with Tahira was like a mystery. She was so unpredictable that I just never knew what I was going to get with her. Some days she could be salty and others she was sweet. And she had been that way since we met.

"You love this dick though, don't cap." I smirked at her before walking off to busy myself with the bookshelf she had waiting for me to put up once I saw her pulling out pots and pans.

A few weeks ago, Tahira bought this bookshelf and it had been sitting there since waiting for me to put it together. I figured since she had an attitude, I'd put it together just to calm her ass down a little.

I could barely think straight with the way she was blasting music throughout her apartment, and I knew for a fact that her neighbors loved when she wasn't home.

"Mm, look at my man hard at work. Thank you, baby." She walked up behind me after she placed my plate on the table. I was just finishing up the bookshelf when she let me know that the food was ready.

"Your food is ready, and you're welcome, with your ungrateful ass."

My stomach instantly jumped in anticipation for the taste of the food she prepared. One thing about Tah Baby she could throw down in the kitchen. Instead of simple chicken and waffles Tahira had to show out. The aroma from the steak, home fries and eggs had my tastebuds watering.

"Thank you, Tah Baby." I stood to thank her and accepted her hug and kiss with pleasure. I looked forward to grabbing a handful of Tahira's ass in my hands.

Tahira was a Dominican Mami I had met uptown about five maybe six years ago. She had a thick Spanish accent when we first met and that shit turned me on something serious, I was on her heels the first day we met, and we were fucking by the third day. We had been locked in ever since. Tah Baby had long jet-black hair that stopped just above her fat ass, Tahira had an ass most females were out here risking their lives for. She was thick in all the right places, and she treated a nigga like a king. What got me the most, what made a nigga weak in his knees most times were her eyes, she had these dark green eyes that had a nigga like me ready to risk it all for her since the very first day that we met. If Tahira wasn't so toxic, I would have wanted nothing more than to settle down with her just vibe but nah, her ass was seven thirty for real.

I walked over to the sink to wash my hands before preparing to sit down and eating my food.

"What?" She must've caught me staring while I stood near the sink drying my hands because she walked over to me with a look of concern written all over her beautiful face.

"Nothing. I can't look at you now?" I asked as I slipped my arms around her thick waist and she pretended as if she didn't want me touching her,

I kissed her lips once and that's all it took for her to switch up.

"You can..." She smiled after she just dipped her tongue in my mouth sloppily and I sat down preparing to eat.

Tahira gave me the look that I knew all too well. She may not have asked me to come over here this morning but she for damn sure was happy that I was came because I had been in the streets heavy the last couple of weeks leaving me with only time to sleep, shit and shower. Come to think of it this would be my first home cooked meal in about three weeks. A nigga didn't even have time to stop by his mom's crib for a plate of food that's how hard I've been grinding.

I was hustling as if my life depended on it because it did. The three-year bid I just came home from took a toll on me and I was on a mission to run it up one more time before I left the streets alone for good. It was time, and not because a nigga was being forced out the streets or anything, life was just too short and I was ready to finally start living, to be honest I been ready, but I didn't choose this life, it chose me, so I had to roll with the punches until I was able to get out, for good.

"Is it not good?" Tahira asked because I was picking over my food, something that I never did.

"You know it's good, I just have a lot on my mind." I admitted before I took another bite of the steak and eggs together and continued to eat until my plate was done.

I remembered a time I didn't ever have to ask for anything to eat because Tahira would just be in the kitchen cooking just because it was one of the things that she liked to do.

"I'm here for you." The sincerity dripped from her voice and truthfully aside from Tahira's toxic ways and behaviors she was a good ass woman. It was just when she got in that mood there was no telling what she was capable of doing, all she saw was red and she'd crash out every time.

Tahira wrapped her small arms around my body and hugged me from behind.

As I stood up from my seat at the table Tahira let me go and I was already knowing what she was trying to do. I could tell from the lusty look in her eyes that she was still trying to get some dick after I came here this morning and hadn't touched her yet. Her eyes lit up once she noticed how hard my dick was through my briefs. Instantly she dropped to her knees ready to devour my dick. She tugged at the waistline of my briefs and freed my dick with a smile. It was long, hard and sensitive to touch once her manicured nails began stroking it and placing lights kisses on the tip. Once she licked the head off instinct I reached down and grabbed a handful of her hair knowing within seconds she'd be swallowing my dick, gagging and everything. Tahira gave crazy head sometimes I'd start some shit with her just to get some head, she thought head fixed everything. If I was sick, head, if I had a bad day, head, if I lost money gambling, head, if I brought her something nice, head.

We just finished making a big ass mess all over her living room and kitchen with her cumming all over her furniture. A nigga was tired, but I knew she would want to clean up before I could even lay my black ass down. While she cleaned up, I threw my clothes on to take the trash out for her and get something from my car.

When I made it back upstairs Tahira was waiting for my black ass by the door with my phone in my hand and from the look on her face I knew it was some bullshit that she was about to start.

"Who the fuck is Gia, Nine?" she asked in a cold ass tone that gave me every reason I needed to leave.

"Yo, give me my phone. Why are you even going through my shit?" I asked, honestly curious to know why her simple ass felt it safe to invade my privacy.

"Why are you texting bitches while you're in my fucking home, fucking me?"

"You really are crazy my nigga, stay out my phone. I don't go through your shit so I expect the same respect in return."

"Respect? You think this is respect? Nine, you don't respect me. Who is that bitch?"

"She's none of your damn business. Put my shit down and go about *your* business."

I couldn't even say that I was surprised when Tahira launched my phone across the room. It was expected because she had a temper on her that wasn't anything nice when she felt disrespected, so I knew she wasn't going for any of what I was saying.

"You wild for that," I laughed because I knew it would piss her off eve more then went to pick up my phone.

"You know what, I'm getting real sick and tired of this same old back and forth. We go through this every two to three months. What are we doing?" Her tone switched up once she noticed me gathering my things to leave.

"Nah, fuck all that, you should have asked me that before you tossed my phone across the room and threw all my shit up here." Her crazy ass had my clothes and shoes that I had here all in the living room waiting for me.

"Know this though, once I take my shit out of here, I won't be bringing it back."

"Yeah right." She waved me off and rightfully so, because she was right, we did this every two to three months and I always ended up coming back. No cap, a nigga was tired of the back and forth.

"Matter fact, keep all this shit. I'm out!"

"I swear you ain't shit, Nine. You want to leave then leave, trust and believe there are niggas lined up to be where you are. Just remember who held your ass down though. Remember who was there for you during that bid when all of them other bitches weren't!"

"We have two different definitions of holding me down. You don't remember how I got sent those pictures of you out with that nigga Tut? Or do you only remember the shit that you want to remember? You funny as hell, Tah."

"I was not fucking him though, I keep telling you that. We were cool, he kept me company, that's that."

"That's that, huh? No funny shit Tah, it doesn't even matter because I still fucked with you after that. On some real shit though, you need to just chill the fuck out sometimes. Throwing a nigga phone across the room and tossing all my shit out is not the answer to your problems when you're just going to get over the situation in a little while. I know what I'm doing here, and what I'm doing with you, I think you're the only one that has shit confused."

"You just want to leave to go be with that bitch!"

"I *just* want to leave before I fuck you up." I smiled at the sight of her sitting there all in her feelings behind her reckless ass actions.

"All you're going to do is call your sisters. You won't do shit."

"And my sisters will fuck you up off the strength of me, you already know that." I shrugged, tight that I was even entertaining her this long. Tahira was scared shitless of Ahja and Rae. Just as much as I didn't play about them, they didn't play about me and neither of them cared for Tahira. She did too much. "You could keep all that shit though. I'm out." I looked down as I contemplated if I really wanted to leave behind the couple pieces of clothes that I had at her crib.

I strolled out her apartment and headed home. On my way there I made a call to Elias to see if he made it to practice okay. When my boy graduated, I was getting him that SRT he had been talking about for months. Elias, Rae, and Ahja were who I went so hard for and my mother of course. They each knew that they could get anything from me.

We can do dinner.

The message from Gia popped up while I was on FaceTime with my little brother, and it put a smile on my face. I had been putting in work just to get her to agree to let me take her out and she had finally given in. That night we spent together last year was faint, I was drunk out my ass, she was drunk, and we were both just living in the moment. Just recently after seeing her at Elias's game I wondered if she remembered that night as vividly as I did. I may have been drunk but I wasn't belligerent. I vividly remembered how she smelled, felt and even tasted.

Everything about Gia was breathtaking and I prayed that she stopped running from a nigga.

"Yo E, hit me when you're done, a'ight?"

"I got you. I think Rae and her boyfriend are going to pick me up tonight."

"Bet, let me know, I'll send an Uber if you need it."

We ended the call the same way we usually did, I let him know that I loved him before I hung up.

I had a crib out in Long Island, that kept me out the way. My house was something I had been saving all my life for. Like most mothers mine refused to leave her crib. My mother was the definition of an independent woman. Even before she and my pops separated, I always witnessed my mother taking care of business. Truthfully even after their separation my pops still took the time to make sure home was good, he was just a stand-up nigga. I grinded since a youngin to have my own everything, my pops taught me the importance of being a man and doing for myself. For my thirtieth birthday all I wanted was to become a homeowner and I made it happen. I had a three-bedroom, two-and-a-half bathroom in Long Island, the reason why my money was low, and I was grinding so hard to get back to my comfort zone. Before I got locked up I just a couple hunnid thou short for a million. Thankfully, my car was in my name, and it was paid off and I had more than clothes and jewelry to show that I was getting money. A legacy was what I hustled for, I was blessed to be able to enjoy my wealth, most niggas were either dead or in jail. And as long as I had air in my lungs, I was going to grind harder than the next man to ensure that me and mine were forever good.

Tahira was blowing my phone up since I left her crib and I wouldn't front, it was hard not responding to any of her text or picking up her calls. I just couldn't keep doing the same thing over and over and expecting different results. Nah, I was ready for a change and Gia seemed like the perfect person to break a nigga out of his old habits.

I checked the time while I got ready for my shower. Gia said that she got off at 4:30 and it was 3:00 now. Eagerly I sifted through my closet thinking of what I would wear tonight. My mind had been on her since the day I saw her at Elias's game.

I hit up Rae and Ahja to see what the vibe was like, I wanted to make sure that she didn't forget a nigga after this.

Take her to dinner,
Phillipe
And please Nine, DO NOT WEAR A SWEATSUIT!
And be nice Nine, she's going through a lot right now, don't be..
you know your usual self. Lol

I read over the messages in the chat with Ahja and Rae and

placed my phone on the charger when I was done with the conversation so that I could shower and head to the barbershop. A fresh cut was mandatory.

I waited a good fifteen maybe twenty minutes before Gia finally showed up. What I can say she was well worth the wait. Her presence turned heads of many niggas and even a couple of females too who were all supposed to be occupied by what was going on around them not her. Her heels could be heard each time they hit the floor as she moved to her own rhythm. I wasn't going lie she had a nigga in a trance. I was almost too stuck to even stand to greet her. Gia was slim yet she was curvy in all the right places. In heels she was almost tall enough to reach my shoulder, like my sisters Gia wasn't but 5'5 maybe 5'6. She was brownskin with a mole on her right eyebrow and dimples embedded in her cheeks. She had light brown eyes that spoke to me before she even uttered a word. I could sense her uncertainty. Gia had this aura to her, it wasn't an innocence in a childlike way it was more like a genuine nature that clung from her with ease. Gia reminded me of a young Gabrielle Union type, she was beautiful.

"I'm sorry that I'm late." She let out with a smile and a wave of nervousness covering her.

"It's all good. I almost thought you were about to stand a nigga up." I stood just to pull her chair out and to get a better look at her sinful curves.

"I almost did if I'm being honest." She hung her head low as she sat down, and I shook my head.

"Damn, it's like that?" I played like I was hurt hoping to bring at least a smile to her face or even lighten the mood.

"I just have my own thing going on... and I didn't want to bring that energy here with you."

"I appreciate that, I'm glad you came." I wanted her to know that I did appreciate her coming out and that I didn't take her time for granted. I felt like I already had odds stacked against me with Gia because she felt like she knew the type of nigga that I was. If you let her tell it, I would end up just wasting her time.

"I need a drink." Gia threw her head back in an attempt to get herself together and keep her composure.

While she took a moment to gather herself, I looked up in search of our server who had come over to the table moments before Gia arrived.

"Good evening, can I start the lovely couple off with some drinks?" Our server was a female with bright red hair and deep dimples.

"Yeah, you can get me a Henny sour and for my lady she'll have..."

"Blueberry lemon drop. Thank you."

"My lady? Nine don't do too much." She rolled her eyes with a playful smile and that was all I needed to see.

There was still a hint of sadness in her eyes, and I knew that look all too well. It was the same look Ahja had in her eyes when she found out that Orin was cheating, and the look Rae had almost every week after being with Greg for a year. I knew now that the pain behind her eyes were behind the actions of a nigga.

"I'm fucking with you. I just wanted to see that beautiful smile."

The service here was faster than what I was used to when I came here the last time. Red head brought our drinks back and took our order shortly after.

"How was your day?" Gia seemed to be loosening up and getting comfortable after a few sips into her drink.

"Long."

"I don't know how you do it, working with them bad ass kids every day."

"I was once of them bad ass kids. So, I take my time with them. Don't get me wrong they can be aggravating as hell, but they aren't that bad."

"You went to high school with my sister, right?"

"Hmm isn't it too late for the getting to know you questions? I already gave you the pussy you don't have to do all that."

"Yo what? You wild for that." I couldn't hold back my laughter at how forward she was being.

"I'm just not for the games Nine... I mean we haven't technically been strangers; I've seen you around, you've seen me around. Why now?"

"Why not now? When you see me, you don't speak, I wanted to change that."

"Because when I see you you're usually with a bitch... I think I should go, I don't have time for another lying ass no-good nigga."

"Who hurt you?"

"Like you care," She rolled her eyes at me like she didn't believe a word that I was saying.

"I care. Sit down and talk to me though. I'm a tough nigga, I can handle your smart-ass mouth but what I don't want you to do is take out whatever that nigga put you through on me. Talk to me..."

"I don't feel like talking..."

"At all or about who hurt you? Because I'm cool with just sitting here in silence looking at your beautiful face."

"Flattery *will* get you far."

"So how about you let me do that for you."

"Do what?"

"Make you smile. I love your smile." I ran my hand through my beard and looked her directly in her eyes as I spoke.

"The ones that make you smile can make you cry..."

"I would never do that intentionally."

"Never say never... Look I like you Nine, if I didn't, I wouldn't be here. Truthfully, I just have a lot of personal stuff going on right now and I would hate to drag you in any of that."

"I can handle it. I just want to make you smile, no strings attached, no bullshit."

"You must have a bitch. That's usually how it goes, the ones that say all the right things are usually the ones with a bitch at home waiting for them to bring their dog ass's home."

"I live by myself."

There it was again, her smile. Gia had a smile that made a nigga weak in his knees. Even if a nigga did have a bitch at home he didn't anymore after getting the chance to sit across from her. "Yeah, whatever."

"Look Gia, all jokes aside, I'm just trying to talk to you and get to know you. I'm feeling you and I'm tired of this whole cat and mouse shit we've been doing. I don't have a bitch. I'm single, yeah, I have a shorty that I fuck with heavy, but that shit could be dead whenever you want it to be. Right now, though, I'm just trying to get to know the woman behind that beautiful smile."

"So just like that you'll leave a bitch that you're fucking with *heavy* for little ol me?"

"Just like that. I'm thirty ma, what I have going on right now is nothing serious. Definitely nothing worth missing the opportunity to get to know you, trust me, if it was, I wouldn't be here. I'm no perfect but I'm not a dog ass nigga. I just don't have time to play games, I spent too much time away to be out here playing games. That's lil' boy shit. If things with us go as I want... never mind, I could show you better than I can tell you."

"Why me?" She blurted out with much concern, and I was already knowing that the nigga she was fucking with before me had her second guessing her worth.

"Why not you Gia?"

She stared into my eyes for a moment as if she was trying to figure out if I was running game or not. I wasn't. I was a man of my word; I lived off morals and principles. I had never had a girl-friend; the streets were always my first love and main priority. Now that I was making money outside of the streets, I was ready to see all that life had to offer and I wanted a lady at my side who was with everything that I was with.

"Nine if we go down this road, the whole getting to know you, hanging out, dating or whatever this leads to, just be honest. I don't need to be lied to or pacified, if I ask you something just be straight up with me and keep your bitch in check."

When our food came, I found myself sitting back and looking

into Gia's very telling eyes. Her beauty was the type that you couldn't deny, I found myself lost in her eyes throughout the night. I could only hope that she took me for my word and accepted that I wanted to get to know her and not play any games. Gia was different from any female that I entertained in the past because unlike many of them she had her own and she was about something. I was used to dealing with women who were fake as fuck with no personalities. Women who thought a silicone ass and titties were they key to a niggas heart and pockets. Gia was different.

In the meantime, we talked more about her job, her dreams and aspirations. Gia loved to dance; she said dancing was what made her feel free. That was something new, something I would have never expected her to say. She had dreams of opening her very own dance studio one day or even just teaching a class. I made a joke about her one day dancing for me, and she waved me off. She told me more about her family, and where she grew up. She did go to school with Ahja and Rae but moved away right before they graduated. I guess that's why I didn't see her around much until that night we got drunk on my birthday.

"Did you graduate from high school?"

"What kind of question is that? You think just because a nigga was in the streets heavy that I didn't have time for an education?"

"No..."

"It' cool, I'm fucking with you Gia. Yeah, I graduated from high school. I have a degree too; my mama didn't play that shit. I would have gone off to be a doctor or maybe even been the next Rich Paul, I love sports and shit, if I never got caught up in the streets there's a whole list of should've, could've and would've-s. One year in juvie happened to turn into two years upstate and then three years in the FEDS for some stupid shit. Altogether I spent six years locked up since I was fifteen."

"You do know that you can still do all that. Your past shouldn't define you, you know. Well, just maybe not becoming a doctor, I don't know if I'd trust you with my health. But I witnessed the way you were with your brother and how excited you seem to get about it. You can still do it if you would like too. It's possible, at least I like to think so. Like who we are right now isn't who we're destined to be."

Gia had me holding on to her word like her word was bond. And for some reason, whatever reason she gave a nigga like me an ounce of hope that everything that I've done in life wouldn't be in vain.

"So, I guess when you get the courage to teach that dance class, I'll get on it."

"Deal." She held her hand out to shake on it with a big smile and I smiled right back at her.

"And I'm serious Nine, I'll hold you to it."

"I like a challenge ma, it's a bet."

We ordered more drinks and talked for hours as I tossed question after question at her which she surprisingly answered with ease. I could sit and listen to her talk for hours at a time, Gia just made the conversation flow with how open she was willing to be with me. I was going to be sure to leave Redhead a hefty tip because she was doing a great job at not interrupting us and only coming when I waved her over for another round.

"Wow I should go; I have to get up for work in the morning."

I nodded without putting up a fight because she had already given me more than enough of her time, I waved our server over and asked for the check.

After our bill was paid, I walked Gia outside.

"I really did have a good time tonight Nine, despite how things started."

"Yeah, you were giving a nigga a hard time."

"For good reason but I'm glad that I stayed."

We spent way more time here than either of us intended to but for good reason.

"You drove?"

"No, I took an Uber."

"Let me take you home then."

"Hmm I don't know if that's a good idea. The last time we were together drunk, I never made it home."

"This isn't that. I can promise you that. We'll have plenty of time for that once I make you mine." I smirked and she playfully rolled her eyes while I led her to my car parked just up the street.

After spending time with Gia, I was already looking forward to the next time we'd be seeing one another. Not once did I worry about the endless amount of missed calls that I received from Tahira tonight. Gia was on my mind all night even after I dropped her off to her crib.

KASH

My life was a fucking movie, and I couldn't make this shit up if I tried. Niggas were steady trying to be me, they tried many times to re-create me and copy my still but there was only one nigga who could do what I do. Even in jail I was that nigga, with my bitch making those monthly trips I was able to get some fire weed in here and niggas behind the wall paid four times the amount it was worth on the street. Only a nigga like me could make fifteen thousand while I was locked up. I couldn't wipe the smile off my face if I wanted to just thinking about the amount of bread I was coming home to and the amount of pussy I was getting into. I wasn't sure what the fuck Gia's problem was, but she hadn't been answering my calls lately, I tried to have my cousin reach out to her, but she blocked that nigga too. If she was fucking with somebody else, I was going to end her and that niggas life. Word to mother.

All I needed to do first was get the fuck out the system so that I could come home and tie up some loose ends. I couldn't wait to shit on every nigga and bitch who counted a nigga out. It was up when I touched the town. My pride wouldn't allow me to be humble, nah, fuck that, I was coming for everything when my time came and each and every nigga that didn't hold it down was on my shit list. Since a young nigga, niggas knew how I gave it up, ruthless. It was always up with me. I couldn't remember a time that I ever ducked smoke.

"Yo my nigga the phone."

"Who that?" I looked up from the floor where I was in push up position wondering what the fuck anybody talking to this bum ass nigga wanted with me.

"My boy Red. He said that word on the street is that your bitch is fucking with some next get-money nigga. Niggas saying you married to Brixx ex shorty. That's true?" From the look on buddy's face, I was already knowing that he was skeptical to the situation. Brixx wasn't a nigga that most niggas wanted to cross or even be at odds with. He was one of them niggas who everybody fucked with I guess.

"Who the fuck is out there with my name in their mouth?" I stood up angrily and snatched the phone, ready to go to war behind a nigga speaking on my name.

"It's shorty. She posted on Instagram and she's walking around with a big ass rock on her finger saying that you gave it to her. That's true?"

I know this bitch didn't use the bread that I sent her to buy some bum ass wedding ring.

"Believe half of what you see and none of what you hear," I responded casually, even though I was fuming on the inside. Neesha was messy and she was going to ruin everything before I even had a chance to touch down with how careless she was going about everything.

I didn't care about Brixx or how he would feel. Neesha was my bitch first, her trifling ass just wasn't loyal enough to stay down for a nigga when I got locked up the first time in 2018. Just so happened, she ended up fucking with my little nigga.

Neesha knew where home was though, so like expected, she came running back the second that nigga left her high and dry. She must've looked me up to get my information about a year and a half ago and we had been fucking around ever since.

Fuck!

When it rains it seems to fucking pour. I thought as I pulled the blunt from behind my ear once I made it back to my cell. Weed was a goldmine in here, niggas were willing to pay anywhere from one hundred to five hundred dollars for a three pointer in here. And luckily, I was the nigga with the weed connect. I had some mid shit and it sold like I had that fye. I knew had I been trying to move this on the streets I wouldn't have made nearly as much bread as I was making behind the wall.

Ever since Neesha got word that I'd be coming home soon she started moving hella fast. We had a plan, and she was going against everything we agreed on. I didn't care for her reckless decisions; I barely even wanted her to be on social media but there was but so much control I could have from behind the wall. Even still a nigga had to do what a nigga had to do to get things done.

The saying "you never really know what you had until it was gone" was true. It was the epitome of my life, from my freedom to my bitch. I wished I treated both with more care. Gia was the only one willing to stick it out with a nigga when it all turned sour. She had been riding with a nigga right or wrong since she was a teenager, she was there through all my highs and my lows and at that time we were just hella cool. We didn't really start fucking around until I got locked up. She had always been there though, even back when I didn't have a pot to piss in or a window to throw it out of.

I had to get my bitch back and get Neesha's crazy ass in check. Playtime was over and I was on the countdown.

"Yo, let me see the phone," I spoke to the lil' nigga who was mid conversation with whomever he was chopping it up with back home.

I didn't have to say it twice before he was telling whoever was on the other end that he'd call them back. And hopefully when I made this call to Gia, she answered.

Voicemail, again... Word to my mother, she could dead all

thoughts of her and whoever that nigga was living happily ever after, because as soon as I came home, I was deading all that.

"Fuck Gia, fuck Brixx, and fuck anybody against me!" I slammed the phone before picking it back up to make a call to Neesha.

"Hey baby."

"Don't fucking play with me, Neesha. What the fuck did I tell you?"

"Kash, it's too early to be arguing with you, for real. Hello to you too nigga, and whatever you heard, I don't even give a fuck. People always seem to run back and tell you shit about me..."

"Bitch, where did you get that ring from? Because I damn sure didn't give it to you."

"I brought it myself, what's the problem?"

"You know what the problem is. We agreed that we were going to keep things quiet until I came home..."

"No nigga, you agreed to that, I didn't agree to a damn thing. What... let me guess, your little bitch found out and now she's mad at you so you're taking it out on me? Story of my fucking life!"

"You need to lower your fucking tone!"

"Kash, I'm not doing this, not today. It's my birthday and you call me with this bullshit? Really? I bought the ring as a promise to myself and yes, I was being petty by posting it on social media on my ring finger, but oh fucking well. You married me nigga, you knew what it was when you decided to say, 'I do,'" she barked, and I wished like hell that we were face to face because I'd probably knock her ass out.

"What you need to be doing instead of focusing on me is focusing on what's important. Brixx is supposed to be getting out the game, so you need to be figuring out how you're going to get your connect back. I told you not to cut ties with him, but you were too in your feelings to hear anything that I was saying."

"That nigga is the reason that I'm even in here. Him and that nigga Eazy, and you expect me to play it cool with them niggas? Nah, fuck them niggas!"

"Listen, now that the cat is out the bag that we're married, Brixx knows that you don't fuck with him anymore anyway, so you need to be in there figuring out what you're going to do." Neesha smacked her lips, only pissing me off even more than I already was.

"Fuck that nigga! Trust and believe, when I come home, I'll be back on top. Don't forget that I'm the nigga who even put him on. That nigga is only eating because of me. I brought him and Eazy outside."

"Well Kash, the both of them niggas are doing better than you despite all of what you just said. You need to let go of the past and focus on what's to come. If you would have just stayed the course and kept your feelings in check for that little bitch, you'd be back on top now... Instead, you allowed your little feelings for that yellow bitch to cloud your judgment and she's out here calling these niggas who set you up 'brother.' You sure know how to pick em..."

"Yeah, I guess so, because not so long ago you were laid up with the nigga."

"Here you go, always bringing up old shit. I only ever got with Brixx in the first place because you were the one who left me. You just one day decided that I was no longer enough and left to fuck with a bitch who left your ass high and dry. If you want to take it there Kash... we can," Neesha snapped, and I bet thoughts of me getting with Bianca, a bitch she couldn't stand, hurt.

"Yo, can you just chill out until I get home? Please."

"Don't worry, Kash, I'll leave your little bitch alone. I really be in my own world and I'm not worried about her. My post got these bitches in their feelings, but you know like I know where home is."

We talked for fifteen minutes more before the phone hung up. I just needed to get home to get things in order. As soon as I got my feet on the ground, it was up. As much as Neesha and I did beef, I knew she was a rider, and she had my back. She would forever be good with me as long as she stayed down. I popped my shit, but I knew what it was. That was my baby.

I just needed a little more time before I was finally free, and I could set my plan in motion. It was crazy how I was the nigga who brought Brixx outside in the first place and now he was sitting right where I was supposed to be.

Brixx and I had known one another since 2012, but as soon as I was graceful enough to put the little nigga on, shit changed. I grew to envy the nigga I introduced to the streets as he grew bigger than me. After just a year Brixx had recruited Eazy and together they had Long Island City on lock while I was struggling to barely take over projects in Brooklyn. That was over ten years ago and now the nigga was way beyond what we started out doing. Word on the street was that Brixx took over my connect and branched off to Houston and Baltimore and that shit had me livid. I hated the fact that he was handed everything that I worked so hard for. It was all me, it was always supposed to be mine, the fame and the fortune that Brixx had in the streets was supposed to just be for me. And what's crazy is the day that I got locked up, Brixx and that nigga Eazy were there. How was I the only nigga to get caught for something that we all did? Shit bust my head for real.

I had a plan in motion though, as soon as I came home, which was very soon. I was going to shake shit up. Brixx wasn't going to know what hit him.

"Miller, on the count," the CO yelled, and I made my way back to my cell.

"I don't know how or why, but your black ass is going home."

I had been waiting to hear those two words for weeks. My release date wasn't for another year, but I had worked out a deal with the DA and received an early release. No one knew, not even Neesha. This whole time I had been moving like I was oblivious to the whole thing.

"You fucking with me, right?"

"Get your shit, you're out of here."

"Damn, I need to make a phone call, let me make a phone call." My bag was already packed. It had been since I spoke with my lawyer a couple days ago. I needed to make a phone call to my cousin Kwan. He was the closest to me and I needed him to set a few things out for me. my lawyer had me thinking it'll be a few more weeks before I was released so I wasn't one hundred percent prepared. Kwan was always on standby though.

I made the call to Kwan about an hour later and now I was playing the waiting game. The Lieutenant said I'd be out of here in the next two hours which meant I'd be back in the towns before midnight.

"What's good my nigga?" My cousin Kwan stood outside waiting to greet me.

"Welcome home my nigga." Kwan dapped me and we chopped it up for a minute before I turned to face the facility, I had been housed in for the last six years with both my middle fingers up.

"Suck my dick!" I yelled before hopping in the passenger seat and Kwan pulled off.

"Where to my nigga?"

"Take me home. I told niggas I'd be back." I smiled proudly.

"I got you. Here." Kwan handed me a phone and some bread.

"Good looking family. You know once I get right, you're first in line to eat with me."

"Just like old times." Kwan nodded and left me to busy myself with my phone.

It felt good to breathe fresh air as a free man. I was finally free!

My mind drifted to Gia and how I was going to fix things, if I was even able to fix things. Gia and I started messing around when I had two years left on my bid. For her to fuck with me while I was locked up spoke volumes. And whenever if ever I needed anything, Gia held it down and made it happen, but Neesha was the one who I could count on to do all the shit Gia wouldn't. Neesha was my down bitch, the one who lived by the code.

"Yo Kwan how long until we get to the hood?"

"About twenty-five minutes."

"Call Neesha for me."

Kwan gave me an odd look, but I wanted to sneak up on Neesha's ass. She was sneaky and it was her birthday so only god knows what she was out doing.

"Yeah Kash." Neesha answered on the first ring already knowing what time it was. It wasn't unusual and I knew she wouldn't suspect anything because Kash would call her on three-way often.

"Yo, I'm sorry about earlier. Happy birthday baby."

"Thank you." She shot back dryly, and I knew she was tight with me.

"You heard me? I said I was sorry."

"Kash I've heard it all before. You're sorry today but tomorrow it will be something else and I'll be another bitch and another hoe."

"Where you at right now?"

"I'm in the house getting ready to go out."

"Nah, I don't want you to go out. I want you to stay in the crib tonight."

"Kash, are you crazy? It's my birthday. It's not like you're here to celebrate with me. I'm going out for drinks with my friends."

"Your hoe ass friends. Why can't your ass just listen?"

"Because instead of being my man, you'd rather be my daddy. And Kash I'm a grown ass woman, I don't need another father, one is enough." She sucked her teeth, and I kept her talking until we were closer.

"Neesh, I love you."

"Mmm, hmm. I love you too, Kash." I hung up quickly because I knew she'd be looking for the operator to cut in any second now.

I gave Kwan Neesha's address and that's where we were headed. We made a stop before we hit the city and I picked her up some roses.

"Yo, good looking, I'll hit you in a few hours, stay close."

"I got you. Tell Neesh I said what up." We dapped and I made my way to Neesha's apartment building with her gifts and roses in my hands.

"Who is it?" she yelled from the other side of the door, and I stayed quiet, placing the roses in the way of the peephole.

"Who the fuck is it?" She snatched the door opened angrily, and that's when I lowered the roses to reveal my face.

"Kash! What are you doing here? You were just in...."

"What? You're not happy to see me?" I asked, slightly offended with the way she was greeting a nigga.

"No baby, I am, I'm just surprised that's all."

"Can I come in or some nigga is in here?" I stepped inside before she could even say another word to check for myself.

"Baby, there is no nigga in here. Just me."

"A'ight then. Happy birthday, these are for you." I handed her the roses and gift bags.

"Thank you so much. I missed you so much." Neesha threw her arms around my neck and her legs around my waist without warning. Thankfully I worked out faithfully because Neesh wasn't petite. She was a big girl, with a phat ass.

"I missed you more." She kissed me sloppily, awakening my dick instantly.

"Happy birthday to me!" she yelled as I led the way to her bedroom with her assistance. I prayed that her pussy was as fire as I remembered it to be. Neesh had good pussy and gave tremendous head. Brixx was the dumbest brotha alive giving her fine ass back to the streets.

"You still going out?" I asked as I rammed my dick into her wetness without warning.

"Mmm baby, I missed this dick," she cried without answering my question.

"You gon' leave me, Neesh?" I asked as I began beating her pussy up.

"No baby, I'm staying, I'm staying... Shit...fuck Kash."

We fucked for hours, and it seemed like she wanted to go for more but there was something I needed to handle still.

"I'll be right back..." I told her as I pulled my sweats up. I showered and threw on a brand-new sweat suit that Neesha had in a pile for me. She had been buying me clothes, jewelry, and shoes since we started back messing around.

"Where the fuck are you going?"

"I'll be right back, chill. Kwan is downstairs and I need to handle something."

"Kash, if you're going to see that bitch, just say that. I knew what this was when I started back messing with your trifling ass."

"You just sucked a nigga dry. I don't have nothing left for no next bitch. I'll be right back, a'ight."

On the ride home, I made a few calls before we got to Neesha's crib, and I got all the information I needed on that nigga Brixx and Eazy. I heard Gia was running around with some new bitch Brixx was fucking with. Ria, Rhia, Rae, some shit like that. My little man's sent me her social media, and it was crazy how much you find out about a person through social media, but Gia nor the other bitch posted enough. So that was a dead end.

"Yo Kwan, pass me the hammer."

The sight before my eyes hurt a nigga's soul. I lost my bitch.

Kwan told me about this lil' spot in Queens that Brixx owned. I wanted to pull up and pop out on the nigga to let him know that the king was back, but the sight before my eyes had a nigga hurting.

"Move from that nigga before I air this shit out, on my momma!"

I sent the text to Gia, already knowing that tonight I was going to have to show my ass.

To be continued...

Made in the USA
Monee, IL
03 October 2023

43894658R00113